D1068071

X
16

DATE DUE

F
LEM

LeMay, Alan
Painted Rock : western
stories

THREE RIVERS REGIONAL LIBRARY
THREE RIVERS REGIONAL
LIBRARY SYSTEM

GILCHRIST COUNTY LIBRARY
P.O. BOX 128
TRENTON, FL 32693

Painted Rock

Other Five Star Titles
by Alan LeMay:

Spanish Crossing
The Bells of San Juan
West of Nowhere: Western Stories

Painted Rock

Western Stories

ALAN LeMAY

Five Star • Waterville, Maine

Copyright © 2004 by the Estate of Alan LeMay

Additional copyright information on pages 210 and 211.

All rights reserved.

No part of this book may be reproduced or transmitted in any form or by any electronic or mechanical means, including photocopying, recording or by any information storage and retrieval system, without the express written permission of the publisher, except where permitted by law.

First Edition
First Printing: August 2004

Published in 2004 in conjunction with
Golden West Literary Agency.

Set in 11 pt. Plantin by Al Chase.

Printed in the United States on permanent paper.

Library of Congress Cataloging-in-Publication Data

LeMay, Alan, 1899–1964.
    Painted rock : western stories / by Alan LeMay.—1st ed.
      p. cm.
    Contents: Whack-ear's pup—Strange fellows—Gunnies from Gehenna—Hard-boiled—Next door to hell—Feud fight—Thanks to a girl in love—Man with a future—Old thunder pumper—The nester's girl—Fight at Painted Rock.
    ISBN 1-59414-000-6 (hc : alk. paper)
    1. Western stories.   I. Title.
PS3523.E513P36 2004
  813′.54—dc22
                                            2004049290

Painted Rock

Table of Contents

Foreword

Early in his career, Alan LeMay observed that fast-paced action stories were timeless. He had attended a high school production of one of Shakespeare's plays and noticed that, despite the amateurishness of the production, the audience was enthusiastic, laughing and applauding the drama. He told me that what appealed to the majority of the public in Shakespeare's time, and at the present as well, was extroverted people involved in action-packed adventures. Western stories fit that concept perfectly. So, knowing little about the West before he moved to California, my father began writing Westerns.

Memorable characters like Old Man Coffee in "Thanks to a Girl in Love" became an essential part of the continuing popularity of his Western stories. They came alive because they were about strong-willed people involved in interesting adventures. Daddy even called himself Old Man Coffee at times, which was probably because he always had a thermos of coffee at hand when he wrote, but he continued the practice by naming my dog Rock, like Old Man Coffee's lion hound.

While most Westerns involved male characters and masculine pursuits, the women that became part of Alan LeMay's stories were strong-willed and outgoing. This may be in part because his grandmothers were courageous women. His father's mother, Karen Jensen LeMay, raised three young sons alone on the Kansas prairie after her husband died at the age of twenty-six, and his maternal grandmother, Elizabeth Carpenter Brown, assisted her husband when he was sheriff of La Porte County, Indiana by cooking meals for the prisoners when she was little more than a teenager.

The character Mora Cameron in "Thanks to a Girl in Love" proved herself a strong-willed woman by working to free her man from the charge of murder, which she knew he didn't commit, and by simultaneously running his mine. Carolyn Clinton in "Feud Fight" was an active character as well as was Willa Brent in "Old Thunder Pumper".

I tried from an early age to measure up to what I felt was expected of me as a Western female, and Daddy was always encouraging. Since he'd worked as a sparring partner for a boxer when he was in college, he tried to teach me some defensive postures and ways to attack that might be useful in helping me to win out over a big girl who was bullying my younger brother Dan at school. I doubt that I measured up to any of our father's heroines, however, because, although I did keep my left up as instructed, my opponent was left-handed, and she succeeded in knocking out one of my right molars. Such an embarrassing thing never would have happened to any of Alan LeMay's heroines.

As an enhancement to the action in a story, Daddy created settings that made the reader feel as if he were present and participating in each adventure. He always visited the locations where his narratives took place, in order to have first-hand knowledge of all the sights, sounds, and smells. He also made friends with cowhands and ranchers to understand better their deep feelings about their land.

Whether he was writing about his unforgettable characters, realistic settings, touching relationships, or powerful drama, Alan LeMay's Western stories always come alive because they are first and foremost stories of adventure.

Jody LeMay Newlove
Pollock Pines, California

Whack-Ear's Pup

The leather-hearted roan, carrying Whack-Ear Banks home at a smooth trot, suddenly stretched down a long nose, snorted, and skittered sidewise five yards.

"What the . . . ?" the big cowpuncher protested. Then, as he cast a swift glance at the cause of the roan's astonishment: "Aw, fer the love o' Pete!"

Swiftly reining in before the gelding could regain his stride, he swung his lean 200 pounds to the ground, and walked back with the reins looped over his arm. The terrifying object was a little, huddled litter of three-day pups.

A chill wind, bearing a foretaste of coming snows, swept down from the mountains, whispering in the sage and rustling the dry stems of the prairie grass. The early dusk of November was pressing down from a sky of frosty lead, giving the vast valley an unfamiliar aspect, unspeakably barren and forbidding. Whack-Ear chafed his cold knuckles against broad palms, and let fall a few scathing adjectives, descriptive of nesters who left little, blind puppies in the middle of 100 miles of prairie to die.

One of the four puppies whimpered, and shivered miserably with the cold. The cowboy cursed with a vivid bitterness, and ended its troubles forever with a merciful blow with the heel of his boot. The rest were already dead.

He now sighted a fifth puppy, a dozen yards away. As he bent over this last of the litter, he saw that the little, shivering survivor was the smallest, the scrawniest, and apparently the feeblest of the lot. His eye estimated the distance that the puppy had crawled, and a shade of admiration crossed the

11

cowboy's big face, that this wretched little runt should still be the only one of them all to struggle against his fate. As he watched, he saw the puppy's strengthless, almost rudimentary legs make yet another effort to propel the potbellied little body forward. Whack-Ear tilted back his Stetson, and ran fingers through his shaggy, mouse-colored hair.

"Game little . . . ," Whack-Ear began, squinting keen gray eyes at the tiny pup. "Poor little son-of-a-gun that don't know when he's through . . . if I don't give you a hand, pardner!"

The cowpuncher stooped and gathered up the pitiful scrap of life in one huge hand. The dog baby lay in the big, calloused palm, looking scarcely larger than a tadpole, so small it seemed, and so weak. For a moment Whack-Ear stood looking at it, while a few hundred yards away a great bull, marshalling a small herd that hulked blackly against the gray of the plain, bellowed in a moaning, deep-chested voice that boomed through the dusk.

The puppy whimpered, a thin, scarcely audible squeak. Whack-Ear opened his shirt, and thrust the puppy inside, against his skin. Then, mounting carefully, he rode on, the roan lengthening his strides toward home.

"Now listen," protested Whiskers Beck, he of the bushy white beard, holding Whack-Ear's pathetic pup in one hand and gesturing with the other. He was a bowlegged ancient, bald as an egg, with smiling blue eyes beneath tangled brows, as white as if dusted with Joe's flour. "You're cook, Joe, an' everythin' centers 'round you. Less'n you help us out, the whole project falls through."

"Leave her fall," said Terrible Joe, so-called in mockery of his inflammable disposition. He thrust out an imposing stomach aggressively, threw back his leonine head, and stared down at Whiskers past a small but bulbous nose. "Do I care?"

"The Triangle R," Whiskers went on, "has been completely dogless fer two years now, or ever since ol' Strap accidentally bit that hot-headed feller in the neck. 'Taint right, not on a up-to-date ranch like this is. If we raise this 'n' up right, he'll be more help than a top hoss on roller skates. Roundin' up cattle, carryin' messages, draggin' in boys that get hurt. . . ."

"Horse collar," said Terrible Joe. "When it's growed, it'll have about a million pups of its own, eatin' us out o' home an' saddle, until the whole works is given over to dogs, complete. *I* know!"

"It ain't that kind of a dog," Whiskers objected. "Jest look at the poor little feller. . . ."

"I won't," declared Terrible Joe flatly, turning a bulging back. "I know my rights!"

He began rattling among his pans.

"Well, I see we got to go ahead as best we can without Joe," said Whiskers, turning to the four other cowboys. "I guess the first thing is feed him."

"What do they eat?" Whack-Ear wondered. "Mush?"

"Somethin' strengthenin' is what's needed here," Whiskers opined. "I never raised no dogs, but I c'n see where this 'n's liable to lose out. We'll take an' chop up some o' that hash, real fine, an' put a little brandy on. When he's wrapped around that, he oughta. . . ."

"Ain't that comin' at it a little strong?" asked Squirty Wallace, a small man, wiry and bowlegged, with a reputation as a top hand. "I'd say he ain't had much practice eatin', so far. His stummick's liable to be plumb astounded. I say start easy, an' leave his belly figger out what it's up against gradual."

"Christ," said Dixie Kane, the slender young bronco peeler, his blue eyes enthusiastic, "meat is what dogs like! A child would know that. Whatcha wanna do . . . make a sissy out o' the dog?"

"You make me sick," snapped Terrible Joe. "Cow's milk, with hot water in it, is what he gets. I got it fixed already. Gimme that cur! I'm the nutrition expert around here!"

Terrible Joe held the pup on its back with one hand, while he tried to pour the weakened milk down its throat with a spoon. The puppy sputtered and gagged, and for a moment the cowpunchers were at a loss. This time it was Doughfoot Wilson who came forward with a suggestion. His slow mind had been pondering the subject for more than half an hour and had reached the correct conclusion at last.

"Put the milk in a bottle," he said, "an' leave him suck it out through a rag."

"Sure, that's right," Dixie agreed. "A child would. . . ."

"Shut up," said Whiskers. "Mebbe a child would, but what of it? Barrin' yourself, we ain't children. Now chaw that, and leave us work!"

For a time, Whack-Ear's pup was a popular dog. Old Man Rutherford, the tall, rocky-jawed chief owner and boss of the Triangle R, had never encouraged dogs. For two years the Triangle R had been untroubled by examples of the breed— unless you considered the prairie dogs called "yaller varmints", or the little, bold, wily coyotes belonged in the general canine class.

Coming into this perfectly dogless environment, many days before he first opened his eyes, the puppy drew a good deal of attention. Until the novelty wore off, the leather-faced cowpunchers used to cut the cards for the privilege of operating the puppy's nursing bottle, at whatever odd hours their work permitted. They named him Splinter, supposing him to have been abandoned by a nester named Jess Wood. As Terrible Joe remarked: "I guess we're stuck with him, all right!"

For a long time Splinter didn't do very well. He was a weak puppy, his system overtaxed by the exposure that had almost cost his life. During the winter months he did little but sleep by the bunkhouse stove—and grow. But how he grew! In the first month he outgrew the old hat that Whack-Ear had given him to sleep in. His skin was loose enough for two dogs of his size, and his paws promised that he would be a big dog, if ever the rest of him got caught up.

Winter passed without other mishaps than those common to small dogs. He stuck his head into a tin can, and could not get it out, until rescued with an axe. Whiskers claimed that his head stuck because he grew an inch while investigating the can. When tied in a given place, he always wound himself up so thoroughly that the only movement possible to him was the rolling of his eyes. Once he was missing for four hours, and was found in a water trough, utterly exhausted from swimming to keep his head up. But these were minor things.

By spring Splinter was half grown, gaunt and lanky after the manner of a hound. With the breaking of the cold weather he began to take an interest in life—and it was then that trouble began in earnest. Such a trail of complications began to be left in his wake that the dingy yellow pup threatened to change the course of Whack-Ear's life.

The first sign of trouble broke when Dixie began to be plagued with fleas. An investigation proved that Splinter had been spending his days in Dixie's bunk. Half a dozen times, at least, Dixie lashed Splinter out of the bunk with his belt, the bronco-peeler's oaths mingling with paroxysms of glee from the other cowpunchers. That Dixie should get fleas was a very merry thing—until Splinter gave up that particular bunk, and tried all the others in turn. The flea epidemic became universal. Splinter was banished from the bunkhouse by common consent.

The banishment of a dog from the place where he is accustomed to sleep is not a thing to be accomplished without sounds of weeping by night. On the first night of Splinter's expulsion, long, sobbing howls went up outside the bunkhouse door. These tearful expressions of grief were interlarded with periods of frantic barking; it seemed fairly obvious that Splinter was afraid of loneliness and the dark.

When it was apparent that Splinter was good for all night, and that sleep was to be a mere figment of imagination, little Squirty Wallace rolled out of the bunk and plunged, cursing, into the dark. There followed a series of sharp *ki-yis*, mingled with the crack of a snapping rope end, and hoarse shouts of wrath. The sounds of pursuit diminished into the distance. Presently Squirty reappeared, breathing hard, and limping painfully from too frequent contact with sand burrs.

Comparative peace favored the bunkhouse, but not for long. A low, wailing sound beyond the door told the cowpunchers that the serenade was about to recommence. Five cowboys and the cook left their bunks with reluctance and bitter words.

"I'll shoot that bastard into little thin ribbons!" bellowed Terrible Joe, brandishing his .45.

All rushed for the door, bumped into each other in a jam at the narrow exit, and then funneled themselves out into the chilly starlight. Here the party lost its effectiveness. The dog was gone.

"Where is the son-of-a-bitch?" Dixie fumed. "Show me that damned dog!"

But Splinter, having correctly understood the confused sounds within, had slunk away to hide.

Several hours passed without further trouble. The cowboys had begun to drop off to sleep when that low, dolorous moan, portentous of bigger and louder things, again sounded without. Six tough men and true raised up on their elbows with one accord. Oaths rumbled in the dark. Whack-Ear heaved his huge body upright and looked toward the door.

"Sit tight, fellers. I'll fix this!"

They heard gentle coaxing outside, and in a moment or two Whack-Ear was again silhouetted in the doorway against the starlight, this time with the wriggling pup under his arm.

"Good! You got him!" burst out Terrible Joe. "Now we'll wring his damned neck!" He jerked to his feet and clutched at the dog with beefy hands.

One thrust of a big shoulder sent the cook sprawling back into his bunk.

"Leave well enough be!" growled Whack-Ear's voice in the dark. "He ain't goin' to howl no more. Some others is, though, if hands ain't kept off my dog!"

Sundry bitter growls replied to this announcement, but no immediate action threatened. Whack-Ear took Splinter into his own bunk, where the little dog wiggled and whimpered softly with delight. And, for the time, that settled that.

Already all hope had been abandoned that Splinter would be of any help in the cow business. Perhaps he was a natural coward at heart, or possibly the bellowing of that great bull, the day Splinter lay a blind and shuddering scrap of helplessness on the plain, had carved into his puppy nature an immutable tale of dread. In any case, Splinter feared cows with a great, overpowering fear. The mere scent of cattle was enough to depress him, and clamp his tail between trembling legs. And the actual sight of a cow, close at hand, always sent him scurrying for cover.

This inherent defect did nothing to increase his popularity

with men whose lives were spent working with cattle. Open contempt was added to the increasing malignance with which the men regarded Whack-Ear's pup.

Whack-Ear, too, was disappointed in the dog whose life he had saved. And yet, curiously, he found the pup to be increasingly dear to him. To Whack-Ear he was still the helpless, whimpering thing that he had once held in the palm of his hand, the game, little runt that had struggled not to die. The hostility of the other cowpunchers had the effect of driving the pup deeper into Whack-Ear's affections.

By the time that the cowboys began riding in for the spring work, it was apparent that Splinter was never going to be a very large dog. He was of an indeterminate yellow color, short and harsh of coat. He continued to be lean and ribby, his ears flopped, and he had the mournful, drooping expression of the hound, but these were his only claims to houndship. His tail was extra long, his paws extra large, but his lower jaw was short and narrow, and he was unquestionably a very small dog. But, although a poor thing, he was Whack-Ear's own. In time of stress, the shaggy-headed straw boss found himself defending the little animal with an impassioned grimness.

Day by day, as the snows melted from the plains, and long strips of green began to show in the brown prairie grass, the cowboys came riding back to their work. Charley Decatur, Old Ben Egan, Geewhilikers Rue, Henry N. Schwatzel, known as "Hankenswizzle" by friends; Joe Harker, Tom Six, Talky Peters, and Blazey Crane of the kinky red hair; Jawn Stewart of the sorrowful eye; Smoky Patterson, who claimed to be the slowest man in the world; Hal Walters, Sam Watson, big Java Lewis, Bad News Grogan, Baltimore Bob, whose last name was unknown; Terry Bryan, Walt Sanders, Highpockets Dyrenforth, and many others came trickling in to round up the remudas, top off their strings, and peel the animal cayuse crop.

As the population of the Triangle R increased, Splinter's opportunities to get into trouble seemed to multiply. One by one, as if with unerring instinct, he was pruning away the last of his friends. Matters came to a head the day that Splinter welcomed the return of Tom Six. Whack-Ear had been away on a five-day ride and was just riding in, jaded and hungry, when the unfortunate event took place. Tom Six, a man with a long, hard face, had unsaddled only a few minutes before and, having been clapped on the back by such cowpunchers as knew him well enough, had started for the mess shack for a hand-out.

Just then Splinter, who had never seen Tom before, discovered the new hand and, for some reason, was seized with instant delight. He leaped joyously upon Tom, ran up Tom's new chaps and clean shirt with muddy feet, and splashed the man's face with a long, wet tongue.

Splinter next touched the ground a good ten yards away, lifted thereto by a smashing kick with Tom's sharp-toed boot. Breathless and stunned, Splinter lay kicking feebly to the accompaniment of strangling noises. Tom stopped swearing and laughed. Whack-Ear dropped from his horse.

In the next moment Tom Six went down under a hurricane of sledge-hammer blows. He was up instantly, and the two big men charged each other with the violence of just wrath. A dozen cowpunchers formed a rooting circle around the battling men, and Old Man Rutherford, anxious to get on with the work, watched with the silence of the resigned. Back and forth and around the circle they fought, with thudding wallops and vicious, smacking jabs. In the end, Whack-Ear won.

When Tom Six had been revived, he rode on to other fields.

That evening a delegation waited upon the big straw boss.

This committee was self-inspired and self-elected, but it had back of it the support of almost unanimous opinion.

"Whack-Ear," said Whiskers, running a purple handkerchief over his shiny head, "me an' some of the boys want to kind o' reason with you about this here dog."

"Which one has the leadin' complaint?" Whack-Ear wanted to know.

"All of 'em," said Whiskers, "an' there's more in the bunkhouse, but the rest o' the boys are newer hands, an' didn't feel they oughta push themselves forward."

"What seems to be the trouble?" Whack-Ear asked.

"Here's just a sample," said Whiskers, holding up a draggled mess that he carried in his hand. "Recernize that?"

"No," said Whack-Ear.

"I ain't surprised . . . how could you? That's what's left o' the purtiest bridle this country ever seen. Light an' strong, with silver all over. I found it in the corner o' the main corral this mornin' . . . chawed, swallered, spit up, an' then tromped on by hosses." Whiskers combed his beard. "Now, I always said give the pup a chance. I wove that collar out o' selected hoss hair, in those colors. But I say he's carryin' this to a ridic'lous extreme."

"I'll pay for . . . ," Whack-Ear began.

"I'm shy one half pair o' boots," said Squirty Wallace, rumpling his russet hair. "An' you know, an' I know, that the guilty party could be spit on plenty easy from here."

He scowled at Splinter, who lolled awkwardly on his haunches at Whack-Ear's heels.

"An' speakin' o' chawed stuff," put in Dixie Kane, "you remember that flame-color contest shirt I had, the one I wore to ride at Pendleton? Best there, wasn't it? It's a thing o' the past now, all right. Just a memory, that's all. There ain't enough left o' that purty shirt to make a mane ribbon for a flea. Look at the little runt! He's laughin'!"

Whack-Ear looked at Splinter and found that Dixie's last accusation seemed to be true.

"The next thing is somethin' else," said Whiskers. "I guess you know that before you rode out we was troubled with a terrible stink in the bunkhouse. Well, it took us a whole day to tear up the floor."

"Some varmint prob'ly crawled under an' died," Whack-Ear said.

"First time I ever hear of a slab o' beef crawlin' under a bunkhouse by itself," declared Whiskers. "Nossir! The varmint that crawled under the floor crawled out again, leavin' that beef behind. An' there he sits!"

He pointed dramatically to Splinter, who rose up to sniff the pointing finger with interest. Whiskers snatched the finger back.

"That hunk o' beef," said Terrible Joe weightily, "ain't the only one I've missed. Not by no means. That dog has a coyote brain!"

"As long as he stole only what Joe cooked up, we might not have kicked," Whiskers went on. "I s'pose you know Madge is back from the East."

He referred to the handsome and hard-riding daughter of the Old Man, a girl of nineteen, beloved of them all.

"Well, sir, Madge cooked up some special pies for the boys . . . bless her heart, . . . an' set 'em on the porch to cool. That damned dog took one bite out o' each an' every pie!"

"I leave it to you if that ain't . . . ," began Squirty Wallace.

"It's sacerlige, that's what it is!" finished Whiskers, getting steamed up. "An' it can't go on! Now we come to some o' the main complaints, them so far bein' jest small affairs. An' I. . . ."

"Listen," begged Whack-Ear. "I'll pay for everythin'

Splinter's done, cash money, notes, or stock. An' I. . . ."

"We ain't askin' that," Whiskers stated. "We want to be
reasonable an' fair. You ain't got enough dough to square accounts, anyway . . . my bridle was six months' pay alone. But
we're willin' to call all bets off, an' leave bygones, bury the
axe. All we ask is that this thing stop!"

"What do you mean?" Whack-Ear demanded.

"Some say shoot an' some say lynch," Whiskers replied.
"But I'm moderate. I say send the dog to some far-off place.
An' I think I can square it with most o' the boys on that plan,
though I may have trouble with some."

"You mean Splinter's gotta be throwed out jest because a
lot o' old maids in overalls says that . . . ?"

"Brother, you named the correct ticket. That dog goes!"

Whack-Ear's gray eyes narrowed. "You're off," he said.
"The man that lays a hand on that dog o' mine will get his
neck wrung with my bare hands! An' the man that hurts the
poor little feller behind my back, I'll say in advance that he's a
yaller, dirty coward, an' a son-of-a-bitch, an' scared to stand
afore me. Any man that thinks o' sneakin' strychnine into
Splinter while I'm gone will have to swaller that, all by hisself,
first. An' I'd a damned sight rather be that yaller dog than the
man that has to know he's swallowed that!"

Whack-Ear turned and left them, stalking off by himself
into the dusk.

Coming in the next day, tired and starved from a hard
day's ride, Whack-Ear noticed the silence that greeted him
with a deep sense of discouragement. This time Splinter
didn't come bounding to Whack-Ear with his usual joyous
welcome. He came crawling, sorrowful and penitent, and
limping slightly from a hectic day of booting and dodging.
But if Splinter could have wept for joy, it was plain that the

tears would have been running down his yellow hide at that time.

The pup whimpered and trembled with emotion as he climbed into Whack-Ear's lap, huddled close, and tried to lick the big cowboy's face. Splinter knew well enough that the world clamored for his blood, and he was ashamed, although uncomprehending of his sins.

Here you are at last, thank God, he seemed to say. *I know I can count on you . . . the only friend I've got!*

The big cowpuncher was moved. "Whack-Ear'll stand by you," he growled, "if I hafta lick every damned saddle-pounder on the range!"

Thereafter, for some hours, Splinter was never farther than six inches from Whack-Ear's heels.

The man's promise to the dog was brought to a test no later than the following day.

Geewhilikers Rue, one of Madge's more fervent admirers, made the girl a present of a baby jack rabbit.

" 'Scuse me, mister," said Whiskers, "but how come a only moderate fast cowboy, such as you be, to catch up with a narrer-gage mule?"

"I got off my horse an' outrun him," Geewhilikers declared.

Whiskers combed his beard. *Think of a knee action like that,* he pondered. *I guess you're hard hit, all right!*

Madge received the infant jack rabbit with squeals of delight that made the bashful Geewhilikers flush with joy. She named the new pet Violet.

Poor Violet, sample of a long-leaping but unfortunate race! While all hands were cheering Dixie Kane's efforts to stay on the hurricane deck of a squealing bunch of steel and high explosive in a cayuse hide, Violet met his fate. Splinter ate him.

Once this casual murder had been discovered, Madge Rutherford wept. In five minutes the news had reached the bunkhouse. Twenty ropes were immediately pledged to the cause of lynching Violet's destroyer. Bullets spurted dust at Splinter's flying heels. Whack-Ear's pup, with a raging gang of cowboys not far behind, leaped through three accurately dropped nooses in his mad dash for Whack-Ear's arms. His owner placed the dog on the ground behind him, where he cowered miserably and peered out from between Whack-Ear's legs. The big cowpuncher confronted the lynching party solidly, with grim death in his eye.

"Gimme that . . . dog!" foamed Geewhilikers Rue, stalking out ahead of the rest.

"Come an' get him!"

Geewhilikers came.

Rue could fight like a wildcat gone mad. Furious fists smashed into Whack-Ear's face. He was driven back against the log wall of the bunkhouse, and his shaggy head banged against a timber. The big cowboy sank to his knees, dazed and blinded.

"Get up! Get up an' get cleaned!" raved the voice of Geewhilikers Rue.

With a great effort Whack-Ear regained his feet. As he reeled forward into another smother of blows, he realized that not one voice had urged him on, not one shout had encouraged or acclaimed him as he struggled to his feet. The ring of watching cowpunchers was silent. They wanted him to lose! A hard thing, that, for a man accustomed to having a loyal outfit solidly at his back.

Whack-Ear fought better, knowing that he was alone. Presently his head cleared, and he began to beat his opponent back with the sheer weight of his heavy, pounding blows. It seemed to Whack-Ear that they fought a long time. He was gasping for breath, his blows weakening, long before he could notice the least abatement of Rue's strength. But at last Geewhilikers went down.

Four times Geewhilikers Rue struggled to his feet and came back for more, and four times Whack-Ear battered him to the ground, until at last Geewhilikers tried to rise and could not. The cowboys lifted him to his feet and, with his arms over their shoulders, carried him away to bathe his bleeding face. As Rue was led away, Whack-Ear heard him demanding thickly: "Leave me go! I can beat him! I can lick him yet!"

Whack-Ear swayed on his feet, his mouth a red smear. "Who's next?" he rasped out. "Step out! Who wants some o' the same?"

No one did. Silently they turned away and left him there, with his bruises and his dog. He slumped down on the bench beside the bunkhouse door. For the first time in many a year the big, amiable cowpuncher found himself deserted and friendless—alone. Silently Splinter climbed into his lap and licked his face.

After the noon dinner, of which Whack-Ear did not partake, Old Man Rutherford called him to his log cottage. Whack-Ear sat nervously, for once, on the edge of a chair in the scrupulously neat room that was parlor, dining room, and office.

"Whack-Ear," demanded the Old Man, thumbing his granite jaw, "how come you can't get along with the boys no more?"

"I dunno," Whack-Ear mumbled.

"They do their work, don't they . . . no fightin' talk nor nothin'?"

"Yep."

"They're good hands, ain't they? Mostly boys we've had every year?"

"Yep."

"You think my straw boss oughta be brawlin' with the hands, an' beatin' up good boys that does their work quiet? You think that's the way to get somethin' done?"

Whack-Ear was silent.

"It's that miser'ble dog!" the Old Man roared.

The cowboy did not reply.

"Who set the mess shack afire last week?" Rutherford suddenly demanded.

"Well . . . Terrible Joe claimed Splinter knocked over a lamp, some way. . . ."

"While stealin' meat," the Old Man concluded. "Look you here, Whack-Ear . . . I don't hold with dogs. A reasonable dog might be all right. But not this here. That dog has got to go!"

Whack-Ear's jaw clamped. "It's a poor man as won't stand by his own dog," he stated. "When Splinter goes, I go, too!"

Old Man Rutherford changed tactics. "Whack-Ear, you got a future with the Triangle R. You own stock now, an' I aim you should own more. Everythin' looks like to work out good for you, if only you don't get some obstinate notion. I'd even thought that in a few years you might. . . ." He hesitated.

Whack-Ear, as if he knew what was in the boss' mind, turned red.

"I was kind o' surprised," the Old Man put in, "that, when a pet belongin' to Madge was tore up, every waddie in the works was mad about it but you. An' you, of 'em all, stood up an' scrapped fer the idea that a little thing like makin' Madge cry didn't 'mount to nothin'. I always thought you was real fond of Madge, Whack-Ear . . . an' she not thinkin' you was exactly poison, neither."

Whack-Ear squirmed miserably. "But . . . but," he stammered, "the poor little feller, he didn't know no better, honest. He wants to do what's right. How can jest a little pup know what he's doin'?"

"Let's be reasonable on this, Whack-Ear," the Old Man urged gently. "Splinter's a real purty thing, an' all, but he's jest a little mite expensive for my ranch. S'pose you'd jest ride over to the Sawbuck outfit, an' make one o' the boys a present o' that dog? They got lots o' dogs there, an' one more won't hurt. An' he won't get in trouble much, because they're used to dog ways, an', anyway, they got so many they won't know which dog done it. You see how things is goin'. Ain't mine a purty fair plan?"

"Yep." Whack-Ear conceded at last. "I reckon."

As Iron Tail, the young sorrel, thrust a careless hoof into a gopher hole and went down, a regret flashed through Whack-Ear's mind that he had elected to ride the most ignorant horse in his string. He had been riding across the prairie at an easy lope, headed for the Sawbuck home ranch, with Splinter clinging fearfully to a position back of the saddle. Suddenly the sorrel somersaulted, and dog and man went headlong into a patch of brush.

Knowing what the half-trained horse would do, Whack-Ear scrambled to his feet, and made a mad dash for the sorrel's reins. He was too late. Iron Tail was up before him, and on his way. Whack-Ear wasted no time, either in pursuit of Iron Tail or in gazing after the horse. He sent one meaningful oath after the receding sorrel, and started back to the Triangle R afoot.

The cowpuncher's chagrin at being set afoot did not convey itself to the little dog. Splinter was only too glad to get his paws on the ground again. He capered, he cavorted, he

barked. He made mad dashes at the solemn-faced little go-
phers, only to have them disappear into their holes at the last
moment with derisive barks. Yet it was Splinter who first dis-
cerned the danger into which Whack-Ear walked.

Whack-Ear had been plodding along with his eyes on the
ground, but he lifted them quickly as Splinter whimpered and
cringed against his legs. Just ahead, three steers, long-legged
critters, lank from scanty winter feed, stood at gaze. The
cowboy slowed his pace and took thought.

Your range steer will not attack a man on a horse. He
knows he will only be made a fool of if he does. But he has
little fear of a man on foot, and he is likely to bear a deep-
seated grudge. Out on the plain the company of steers is not
always a very wholesome thing for a horseless man.

Add a dog to the combination—steers hate dogs. The
sight and the scent of them stir the bovine heart to wrath.
Doubtless the cow mind confuses dogs with coyotes and
wolves, with which they have a permanent war. At any rate,
cattle can think of nothing else while there is a dog in sight.

Certain trouble was ahead. The group of steers was directly in Whack-Ear's path. He considered circling around
them, but realized that with Splinter as a magnet the attempt
would be futile. He reached for his holster, to see that his .45
was loose and ready for work. As his hand touched leather, a
great shock ran up his arm to his brain. The gun was not
there.

He knew well enough where it was. It was in the patch of
brush in which he and Splinter had landed when Iron Tail
fell. He cast a swift glance back over his shoulder, cursing
himself for his carelessness. The patch of fresh brush was now
a quarter of a mile away.

Whack-Ear had his choice of two ways. He could rush the
steers, hoping that they would flee, or he could back off,

trying to reach his gun before the steers should approach and make up their minds to rush. He chose the former.

"*Yip-yip-yip-ya-whoopee!*" he yelled. "*Eeeyahoo!*"

Waving his hat, he bounded toward the cattle. The three steers gave a little ground, then lowered their heads and stood, waiting. Still yelling, Whack-Ear diminished his strides and stopped, perhaps fifty yards from the three steers. Then he fell silent. Thus confronting each other, the two parties stood, the three steers and the man with the dog. For a full minute the five stood in motionless silence, waiting for the next move.

One of the steers pawed the ground, showering his back with clods of the moist turf. He began the rhythmic, deep-chested groaning that precedes the bellow, and Splinter, trembling violently, whimpered until he almost sobbed aloud. The deep, moaning voice broke into the bleating soprano blare of the challenge. The situation wasn't improving much.

"Splinter, go home!" Whack-Ear ordered.

He knew that the steers would never catch a running, dodging dog, and that in Splinter's departure lay safety for them both.

"Go on! Go home! Git!"

Bewildered by this apparent abandonment, Splinter shrank the closer to the ground, huddling as near Whack-Ear's legs as he could. The cowpuncher saw that there was no hope there. The pawing steer, a great white-face, moved two steps forward, and paused.

Whack-Ear began to move away. Slowly, trying to conceal the fact that he was moving at all, he walked backward, stepping clumsily in his high-heeled boots. The steers followed him suspiciously, a step at a time. Slowly Whack-Ear gained a little ground, a little more, a little more. . . .

Suddenly the steers surged forward. Whack-Ear yelled, and once more they slowed to a stop. He realized what had happened. Splinter, although keeping close to his master, had momentarily turned tail. The eyes of the steers were on the dog, more than on the man. The pup was spoiling the bold front that was their only hope. The man swiftly stooped and caught Splinter up under his arm. He could feel the little dog trembling against his side as he again backed off. The critters had closed ten yards.

Whack-Ear was saving his voice now. It was his only weapon, and he must use it seldom, lest it have no effect when it was needed most. The three great, expressionless heads stared with a peculiar blank fixity, as if with eyes of glass. When they stood motionless at gaze, the cowpuncher moved backward. When they walked forward, the man stopped, waved his hat, yelled, leaped into the air—anything to puzzle the dim cattle minds, and halt that deadly, implacable advance.

He glanced over his shoulder at the distant patch of brush where he knew his weapon lay. So little distance had he covered that his objective seemed no closer at all. And when his eyes struck back to the cattle again, they were just a little nearer than before. It was at this point that fear came into Whack-Ear's mind. His imagination pictured the final, irresistible charge, the flashing hook of horns, the stabbing grind of trampling hoofs.

A swift panic swept through him, and a savage desire to turn and run. He took time to steady himself, for he knew such a move would swiftly accomplish the end.

He backed away again, and again the cattle followed. They had closed another ten yards now. Hardly thirty paces separated the cattle from the retreating man and dog. Once Whack-Ear lost a yard or so in another futile effort to drive the cattle back. Again a clump of sage unsteadied his backward stride, and the steers had surged nearer before his balance was recovered.

Unlimited time seemed to pass as Whack-Ear made his slow, losing fight for ground. The sweat stood on the cowpuncher's face, although the breeze seemed cold at his back. He glanced over his shoulder again. He was a little nearer now. He had come—a third of the way? Hardly. A quarter, perhaps. And the cattle had closed the distance between them a little more. Twenty-five yards now. They were coming again. Now the interval was a little less.

The critters were becoming bolder. They no longer stopped suddenly at his yell. He could stop them, but their long strides seemed to eat up the ground at each advance, nor did they always stop at the first yell, or the second, or the third. They knew now that a leap into the air meant no harm, and that there was no danger in a swinging hat. Only instinctive caution in the presence of man and, perhaps, the knowledge that their enemies could not get away, were holding them back.

They were twenty yards away, yet it seemed that the distance to that patch of brush had not appreciably decreased. Whack-Ear wondered if, after all, he could find his .45 quickly enough, even if he were there. They were coming on, and he made weird motions and yelled. Gradually they came to a stop. They were eighteen yards away . . . fifteen.

It was a hard thing to stand still when the steers advanced, yet it must be done. Better that they close the distance a little, than that they not be stopped at all. For a long time Whack-Ear kept himself from looking over his shoulder. He made his way backward, always facing the steers, retreating foot by foot until it seemed that surely he must have come most of the way. Then he looked. He had come halfway, but the steers were very close. The leading steer pawed, voicing persistently those deep, ominous moans.

Fourteen yards separated man and steers. Thirteen. Twelve. Every time he was forced to pause to front the steers, the cowpuncher lost a little more ground. He realized now that he would never reach the patch of brush in time. Splinter trembled, and seemed to cling to Whack-Ear with his paws. His warm tongue suddenly licked the man's hand. The man clutched Splinter closely as he thought of Tom Six, and knew what that hard-eyed cowpuncher, placed in a similar position, would do.

Calmly, now, with his fear in the past, Whack-Ear waited for the inevitable crisis to come. Not for an instant did he relax his efforts to gain ground. He sought desperately for some new strategy, some impossible feat of resourcefulness that would in some way delay the end. But in the back of his mind he knew that there was no longer any hope.

Twelve yards, then eleven. Ten. He could see every swirl of hair on those broad white-faces with the staring eyes. He wondered why they did not rush, how it was that he could still hold them back when they were so close. Then, suddenly, the long game came to its end.

Stepping backward in a long stride, Whack-Ear trod on ground that seemed to collapse beneath his foot. A gopher hole, such as had been the beginning of his trouble, was now apparently the end. Desperately the big cowboy sought to regain his balance as he went down, but could not.

He heard the snort of the steers, the sudden wild trample of hoofs, and caught a glimpse of horns and eyes that showed the whites. All this as he fell, flinging Splinter from him. Swiftly Whack-Ear rolled toward the drumming hoofs, thus escaping the reaching, hooking horns. He felt a hoof drive through the flare of his chaps, and another grooved his arm.

Hoofs stumbled against his body, battering him mercilessly. Yet somehow he escaped, and the trampling thunder passed on.

The three steers plunged on many yards, carried by their own momentum. Whack-Ear saw them stop, sliding on braced legs in the moist footing. They turned, and for a moment hesitated with heads up, puzzled that they had somehow missed their mark. He considered getting to his feet to face them again. He thought of dodging, in the hope of obtaining a bulldog hold. Had there been but one or two, there might have been a chance. But he lay still, hoping that they would follow Splinter.

Then they sighted him, and snorted as their heads went down. The clods flew from their heels as they lunged forward into the charge. The lust of battle had heated their blood; there was no facing them now, no chance at all, except for the desperate, fleeting one that lay in trying the rolling trick again. Whack-Ear hugged the ground, watching. At the exact instant before they hashed him into the ground, he would roll into that mad flurry of hoofs, hoping to make them miss.

But they did not pass over. The foremost critter came to a sliding stop, and the great head came down. Whack-Ear shifted his position like a cat, and a sweeping horn cut the ground where his body had been. He was between the horns. The massive forehead jostled his back as the steer sought to worry him. The sod ripped on either side, but for the instant the animal's very nearness saved his life.

The other two had passed on, pursuing Splinter perhaps. He heard them rushing back. He heard Splinter give a little yelping gasp of fear, almost in his ear. Then, suddenly, the steer above him flung up his head with a whistling snort, and whirled away from him. Whack-Ear, still hugging the ground, turned his head to look. An amazed thrill shot through the man.

Splinter had the steer by the ear.

The cowpuncher saw the little dog clinging with his teeth as the steer bellowed and shook his head. For a moment Splinter's grip held, then, the ear tore into ribbons, and the dog was flung to one side. The great animal reached Splinter in a bound before the dog could gain his feet. The horns tossed in a hooking sweep, and Whack-Ear saw the little yellow form spinning through the air.

The other cattle were with the leader now. A second critter was on Splinter almost before he touched the ground. Again the lunging hook, and the little yellow body turned in the air above the horns. Whack-Ear ripped out a wrenching oath and, struggling to his feet, dashed after the steers.

Suddenly a furiously ridden horse cannonaded into the group of cattle, crashing headlong into the leading animal. Horse, man, and steer went down, the horse somersaulting and the man flying free. The rider was in the saddle again as the horse scrambled up. A second rider—Whack-Ear recognized the faded red shirt of Whiskers Beck—dashed up with a *"Whoop-hi-yah!"* and his snapping rope made the fur fly from a broad white face.

The steers fled. The first horseman—Dixie Kane, to judge by his methods—overtook the hindmost steer, seized the tail, and threw the animal headlong. Whiskers, having ridden in pursuit long enough to get in a few more cuts with his rope, stopped his horse and opened fire. Three times his gun spoke, but except that a shattered horn flew spinning, leaving a smear of blood in its place, the shots took no effect.

Whiskers and Dixie Kane came riding back.

"Well, anyway, I took a handlebar off one!" Whiskers remarked.

Whack-Ear was kneeling by the battered form of his little dog. The others dismounted, and stood beside him. The three made a swift examination.

"He's alive," said Whiskers. "He's breathin'."

"His shoulder's tore open clear to the bone," said Dixie Kane.

Whiskers silently jerked off his neckerchief, and with this Whack-Ear clumsily bound up the wound.

"Don't seem to be anything broken much," Whiskers said at last.

Presently Whiskers produced a flask, and tilted a mouthful of snake-bite remedy down Splinter's throat. At this the little dog coughed, sneezed, and tried to lift his head. Three cowpunchers heaved a sigh of relief.

"If he hadn't come back fer me," said Whack-Ear dazedly, "they never would o' got him."

Whiskers nodded.

Presently, after Dixie had found Whack-Ear's horse, the two cantered on home. Whack-Ear followed at a walk, carrying Splinter in his arms.

As Whack-Ear reached the Triangle R, he rode straight to the corral. He placed Splinter gently on the ground and found that the dog was able to walk some. Then he changed his saddle and bridle to the roan, the horse that he owned himself.

Next he rode to the bunkhouse, gathered everything he owned into his bedroll and war bag, and lashed them onto his saddle. Lastly, carrying Splinter, he led the roan to the Old Man's cottage, and walked in.

Old Man Rutherford sprawled in a homemade chair, smoking a reflective pipe.

"Mister Rutherford," said Whack-Ear shortly, "I've

changed my mind. I quit. Gimme my pay, an' I'll ride."

"No," said the Old Man.

"I don't feel like arguin'," Whack-Ear said. "Where Splinter goes, I go, too. If you don't wanna pay me now, I'll let you know where I'm at, an' you can send my check later."

"Whack-Ear," said the Old Man, "a couple o' the boys has beat you here. Dixie an' Whiskers . . . especially. Whiskers . . . has told me a big lie about your dog pullin' a steer offen your back."

"It ain't a lie," Whack-Ear said.

"Lie or no lie," conceded the Old Man, "they used to be plumb against that dog, an' now they're for him. They swear to high heaven that their yarn is true. An' the way the boys is stringin' over onto Splinter's side, it looks like I can't run this show without a dog no more."

The day's bother had shaken up Whack-Ear's mind. For a moment he stood there, looking foolish. Then Splinter whimpered, and Whack-Ear, who had been carrying the dog in one arm, sat down on a chair, to make the pup more comfortable.

"So we'll have less of this nonsense," said the Old Man. "Damn it, you *got* to stay."

There was a tentative rapping on the door.

"Come in!" roared Old Man Rutherford. In came Whiskers Beck.

"I just wanted to say," he offered, "that the boys have took up a little collection of about seventy-one bucks, in favor o' Splinter, an' we figure to buy him a suit o' dog clo'es, or somethin'. Think it out an' leave us know what he'd like."

He started to go out, but at the door he turned, and came back.

"Say," he began again, "I saved the silver *conchas* offen that bridle that . . . that had that accident that time. Mebbe they'd look nice on Splinter's collar, huh?"

Strange Fellows

He was a wanderer in all kinds of cow countries, a drifter, a floater, homeless yet always at home. In his twenty-six years he had ridden on both sides of the Divide for many owners and in many states. He knew the ways of Texas, of Wyoming, of Idaho, and Montana. But especially he knew the ways of horses and of men. His name was Dan Torkaway.

As long as a horse and the vast open and scattering range were his, he wasn't troubled to know what it was that was always calling him elsewhere, forever leading him on. Lately, as it happened, there was also something driving him from behind. And so, working here and loafing there, he arrived at the clustered log buildings of the Triangle R, as many a cowboy had from time to time in the past.

The boss and chief owner of the Triangle R, tall and rocky of jaw, with keen gray eyes that squinted between muscled cheek bones and grizzled brows, was sitting on a box, watching a pair of fence-building Mexicans work. He turned as Dan Torkaway approached and appraised him with a casual survey.

He saw a sandy-haired cowboy of middling size, with a lean, smooth face beneath a traveled hat. A slender scar ran down the right side of his face, paralleling the smile lines that carved the leathery cheeks. There was nothing conspicuous about the rider's overalls, faded blue neckerchief, and weathered gray shirt. The chaps were a little more striking, being of bald leather, each studded with silver *conchas* along the edge of the flare. He rode an ordinary bay gelding with the hill pony's whiskered jaw, just another cold blood, such as most.

But the horse that Torkaway led held Rutherford's eye longer than the man. This second horse was a black, as magnificent a stallion as Rutherford had ever seen, a tall, clean-limbed animal with compact hoofs that placed themselves accurately and spurned the ground with brisk, springy steps. The neck was conspicuously arched for the Western country, where most horses carry their heads level, saving their energy to travel far, and the big eyes were curiously light, like pale agates, with a ready tendency to show the whites.

"Mister," said Torkaway, dismounting, "maybe you can tell me who's the bull with the brass collar around here. Rutherford? Is that the handle?"

"Talkin'," said the Triangle R's Old Man.

"Name's Torkaway," said Dan. "Any ridin' to do? Lookin' for some."

"Torkaway," Rutherford reflected, getting up. "Seems like I heard of another waddie name o' that some place."

"Got as much right to it as he has, I reckon."

"I s'pose. About the ridin', I dunno. Too bad you weren't here for the fall drive. I ain't exactly organized for the winter yet. S'pose you stick around for a couple o' days, an' we'll see what works out."

"I'll sure do that," said Torkaway, "an' much obliged."

"Good-lookin' horse, there."

"Yeah, he's. . . . Look out!"

The warning would have been too late. The black whirled like a coiling rattler. At the same instant Rutherford took three long, almost unbroken steps backward out of range of the ready heels. Realizing that his move had failed, the great black gracefully spun about again to face the men and stood waiting.

"Liable to do such," Torkaway said gravely. "Thought I noticed him takin' your range."

"I allow that horse has caused bother from time to time?" Rutherford suggested.

"Yeah?" drawled Torkaway. Rutherford now noticed that Torkaway's green eyes were peculiarly shallow and cold, as if just back of them stood weathered limestone walls. Then, after a moment: "Yeah," said Torkaway more amiably.

"Might you trade?"

"No," said Torkaway.

"Well, haze 'em into the corral. The cook's name's Joe. He'll hand you out somethin' if handled right."

Dan Torkaway grinned. "Thanks."

Rutherford's eyes followed the man until he disappeared around the corner of a log building, then the Old Man turned away and strolled toward the bunkhouse. Something was troubling him in the back of his mind, lurking in the shadows that his memory could not quite pierce.

"Torkaway," he muttered. "Torkaway. Now where the hell did I hear that name before?"

Within the bunkhouse Squirty Wallace, wiry little top hand, was lining his bunk with old newspapers. Whack-Ear Banks, the shaggy-headed giant of a straw boss, sat on his own bunk opposite, smoking a hand-made cigarette and offering advice.

"Friend Squirty, he figures it's just about the dead o' winter," he told Old Man Rutherford as the latter stepped inside. "Whiskers, he left a old calendar around an' Squirty found it. January says the calendar. So right away Squirty knows he's 'most freezin' to death. But he ain't one to ask fer a extry blanket, not Squirty. No such dude frills fer him. Give him plenty o' newspapers, says he, an' he guesses he'll make out."

"I got my eddication," said Squirty, standing up squarely on his bowed legs to twirl a cigarette into being, "by spending my nights over literchure, an' there ain't a newspaper in the country that ain't found my infloonce to be pressin'. Also, I ain't like one feller I know that puts everything off to the last second. 'Course, some can't learn, but long experience has showed me that it sure gets cold in the winter. I know one feller," he went on, turning back to his task, "that always is plumb surprised to find winter come around again, same as last year. Come a hard freeze, an' he crawls out of his bunk pretty near froze stiff. He guesses he's got rheumatiz. He guesses he won't be able to ride much today. He wisht he'd known he'd need a overcoat this year. Why didn't somebody tell him it was goin' to be a cold Christmas?"

"If you old ladies will leave me get a word in edgeways," said Old Man Rutherford, "I started to let out that there's a new feller rode in. I ain't exactly took him on yet. Might. See if any o' you boys know him, an' if there's somethin' spooky about him, leave me know. Dan Torkaway's the name."

"Dan which?" said Squirty.

"Torkaway. He has a horse."

"Ain't that nice," said Whack-Ear who could get funny with the Old Man. "Not a real live one? Now, who'd 'a' thought . . . ?"

"This is a real horse," interrupted Rutherford. "Mebbe you should take a look at him jest to see what a good one is like."

"Guess the Old Man's gettin' particular about who he has us associate with," commented Whack-Ear when Rutherford had gone. "Did you ever hear tell o' the like?"

"That new hand sure must be a mean-lookin' *hombre*," agreed Squirty.

He spread out more paper, then suddenly paused over a yellowed, tattered old sheet.

"Found a pitcher?" asked Whack-Ear.

"Just lookin' at the weather report," said Squirty, running a hand through his rusty hair. "What was this stranger's name, now?"

"Dan Torkaway," said Whack-Ear, "as I heard it."

Squirty Wallace casually folded up the yellowed old newspaper and stuck it in a back pocket.

"Never heard of him," he remarked.

"I thought you better save out somethin' to read," said Whack-Ear. "You're right in savin' the oldest one, too. It's liable to wear out on you. You can get the late news out o' them others some other year, after they're more seasoned-like."

"Whack-Ear," said Squirty with gloating malice, "there'll come a time when you'll jest beg me with tears in your eyes bigger'n cartridges to leave you see this news item I got here."

"What is it?" demanded Whack-Ear with sudden curiosity.

"You go to hell!"

Limpid twilight settled like a magic spell of peace upon Wyoming. The light of day slowly dissolved, seeping away over the edge of the world in a glory of silver, purple, and red-gold of such beauty as to hurt the hearts of men. There was the great silence of vast spaces, a silence that was somehow as clear as the voice of a silver bell. Very small in the vastness of mountains and plains, the log buildings of the Triangle R nestled among their cottonwoods, touched with the crimson of the setting sun.

On the bench before the bunkhouse five cowpunchers lounged in attitudes of rest, smoking in silence for the most part, their eyes on the far away. The blue smoke rose in slender, smooth threads from the glowing coals of their cigarettes.

Dan Torkaway silently went into the bunkhouse and came out with a small banjo, produced somehow from the complicated folds of his bed. He tuned it softly, and presently began to sing in a mournful tenor voice to the accompaniment of minor chords. The words of the song went something like this:

> Oh, I ain't gonna ride no more, never.
> I ain't gonna ride no more.
> You can't find flapjacks in a sandstone ledge.
> Cows are all right, but they don't lay eggs.
> It's hellish hard walkin' when you've broke your legs.
> I ain't gonna ride no more.

"Now that's what I call a real philosophical piece," commented an ancient cowboy whose shiny baldness of head was in some part compensated by the enthusiasm of his brushy white beard. It was Whiskers Beck, aged dean of the Triangle R's boys. "There's a lot of truth in that song. Leave me get my mouth organ, an' I'll jine in."

With Whiskers playing a syncopated tenor on his mouth organ, they went on:

> I got me a horse, name o' Woggle-Eye Jim,
> He couldn't ride me, so I had to ride him.
> I had another horse, name o' Pickle-Foot Bill,
> He wouldn't leave me off him, so I'm ridin' him still.
> Oh, I ain't gonna ride no more, never.
> I ain't gonna ride no more.
> Never tie your horse to a prairie dog pup.
> You can't pull up a post hole, it splits all up.
> Fallin' off's all right, but you stop so abrupt.
> I ain't gonna ride no more.

"Now I swear," said Whiskers, "this here harmony's jest plain wasted on these roughnecks here. I move we take our act up to the house where it has some chance to be 'preciated. Madge likes music fine."

"Lead out," agreed Torkaway.

"I got a mouth organ, too," said Dixie Kane, the bronco peeler.

He smoothed down his hay-colored hair and tagged along.

Old Man Rutherford sat in a tilted chair on the porch of his little cottage, his boots on the rail. Madge, his nineteen-year-old daughter, sat beside him, her level gray eyes dreaming into the distance. She was wearing a starched red-and-white gingham dress in contrast to the overalls she wore during the day.

"We come to sing you a song," said Whiskers quaintly.

"Guess we can stand it," Rutherford grunted.

Whereupon the three sat down on the porch step. For a moment Dan Torkaway peered through the shadows at Madge, his fingers wandering idly over the strings. Then, after a little thought, he played a few chords and began to sing. Whiskers trailed in with the extra accompaniment.

Long are the trails, honey, rough are the ways,
The rocky trails I've rode since the old, old days.
Many are the spots where my campfire's shone,
Gleaming in the quiet of the All Alone.
Still my dreams take me back to long ago,
When first I went ridin' out of old Alamo.

"Where was you, Dixie?" Whiskers asked.

"I just got this, an' I ain't quite learned to play it yet," the bronco peeler admitted. "But didja hear the way I come out on that last note?"

"Chorus!" Whiskers announced, getting his mustache over the mouth organ again. Dan went on:

> **I can't think o' nothin' but your eyes so gray,**
> **Shinin' like the east at the break of the day.**
> **All I remember is your pretty brown hair,**
> **Softer than the mist in the starlight there.**
> **All my thoughts are in the long ago,**
> **When I went ridin', ridin' hard, ridin',**
> **Ridin' out of old Alamo.**

"Last time I heard that ditty," said Dixie, "seems t'me like it spoke of 'your eyes so blue' to rhyme with 'flowers in the dew'. It also said . . . 'purty yaller hair, shinin' like gold in the star . . .'."

"Aw, shut up," said Whiskers.

"Mebbe you should sing, an' me play the mouth organ," Dan suggested.

"Oh, no," answered Dixie hastily. "You're doin' fine. I didn't say nothin'."

Down by the bunkhouse Squirty Wallace moved restlessly and went to squat on his heels beside Whack-Ear.

"Ain't he never goin' to quit singin'?" Squirty growled.

"Why, the boy ain't only jest begun," replied the big straw boss. "You jealous, Squirty? I think it's real purty."

"*Humph,*" said Squirty, and lapsed into silence.

"I've seen this ranny before," said Whack-Ear presently. "He was in the act o' bein' shot at."

Squirty turned his slow, steady brown eyes on Whack-Ear and waited inquiringly.

"I was crossin' the street towards Jake's Place in Tonca,"

Whack-Ear went on. "Torkaway rode up jest then on that big black man-eater he's got here, an' I stopped right there in my tracks to look at that horse. Just as Torkaway fixes to climb down, the livin', spittin' image of hisself comes out o' Jake's Place."

"The spittin' image of who?"

"The spittin' image of Torkaway. Listen, will you?"

"You mean, the two fellers looked alike?"

"Squirty, I think you're beginning to get the idee. Well, for a minute they freezes there, starin', same as if each one had met himself an' couldn't figure it out. Then the feller on the ground grabs out his iron an' throws down on Torkaway. *Bam-bam!* An' friend Whack-Ear Banks sure plasters hisself flat in the dust, me bein' somewhat in a general line with the unfriendliness."

"Never mind about you. What'd Torkaway do?"

"He slaps the steel into the big black, an the black purty near jumps clean out from under him. I never see man an' horse leave any place quicker."

"Didn't he fight back any?"

"Oh, he tried a shot or two on the run . . . from a good ways off. An', mister, the closest thing those shots came to . . . was me!"

"Well, then what?"

Whack-Ear looked pained. "Why, that's all. Whatsamatter? Ain't that a good story?"

In the pause that followed, Torkaway's song came to them across the intervening space, a dolorous song with Spanish words.

Qué es la vida, un frenesí . . .

Beneath the lamenting voice, the banjo pulsated a song of

sorrow of its own in minor keys.

"What's he singin' at her?" demanded Whack-Ear suspiciously.

"Jealous, huh?" taunted Squirty in his turn. "He 'lows as how life is a hunk o' cheese, s'far as he's concerned. That's all. Never mind that. You mind that newspaper I saved this afternoon? Piece in it about the Torkaway boys."

Whack-Ear sat up.

"Three years old," Squirty went on, "but news yet. Did you ever hear tell of a horse called Iron Paws?"

Suddenly Whack-Ear snapped his fingers. "I got it now. That's where that name Torkaway come in. Killer named Iron Paws got Old Man Torkaway down Arizona way. Three-day mystery about it because Old Man Torkaway's horse went home to another ranch with blood on the saddle an' somebody found a bloody glove with black horse hair caught in the buckle, Torkaway's horse bein' a sorrel."

"I didn't know that part."

"Turned out that Old Man Torkaway had been killed by this Iron Paws right in sight of one of his sons. An' they jest buried him without any remarks until folks got 'round to askin' questions. Whereupon the boys answered the questions, an' that was all."

"Not quite all," said Squirty. "There was somethin' funny about it. Such that the coroner pretty near had Old Man Torkaway dug up to take a look-see himself."

"What kind of funny?"

"I dunno. The paper jest said that the notion to dig up Old Man Torkaway had been called off owin' to the feelin's o' both boys. An' Iron Paws was shot by Daniel Torkaway, Old Man Torkaway's younger boy."

They fell silent, and heard the end of Dan Torkaway's song.

Todes los hombres sueños son.

An off-key squawk from a mouth organ trailed into the night after the banjo had died away. They heard Dixie's— " 'Scuse me. I dunno how I done that."—and Madge's laugh, a satisfying laugh, somehow suggesting the rich, full flavor of homemade bread.

"Squirty," said Whack-Ear softly, "it was Dan Torkaway's own brother that pulled down on him down Tonca way, surer than all. . . ." Suddenly he growled thickly, getting to his feet. "That son-of-a-bitch has got no right to be singin' to Madge!"

"Wait!" urged Squirty, gripping the big man's arm. "What you goin' to do?"

"Try to get 'em away from there. Hey, Whiskers!"

"Yo!" came from the porch of Old Man Rutherford's cottage.

"Tenspot's worked his way out o' the corral!" bellowed Whack-Ear.

A pause, then Whiskers's voice from the porch: "You tell that fool hoss I said to go right back in!"

Whack-Ear's neck thickened.

"I'm goin' up an' pull that Torkaway killer off o' there by his neck!" he growled.

Squirty Wallace planted himself before the big man in a way that endowed him with an air of unlimited authority.

"Now, wait," he insisted, gripping Whack-Ear's arms. "Let's us go off an' talk this thing over, you an' me."

And Whack-Ear suffered the bowlegged little top hand to lead him away.

Leaning against the heavy poles of the main corral, Whack-Ear cooled off somewhat and rolled a careful cigarette.

"You know what?" he said wonderingly. "That Torkaway killed his own pa."

Squirty considered. "How d'you figure?"

Whack-Ear's eyes stared narrowly at nothing while his big fingers rolled the cigarette between them. "Look. Old Man Torkaway gets himself killed. His boys bury him quiet, givin' out that Dan Torkaway seen him killed by a outlaw horse. All we know is that the signs showed that a black horse was at hand right then, there bein' black horse hair caught in the buckle of Old Man Torkaway's glove. But the coroner, he knew somethin' else. Somethin' downright suspicious-lookin', because no one wants to go pokin' into graves without they got a fine, large reason. Somehow the boys get that investigatin' called off.

"All right. About a year after that I see both boys in Tonca. Now, look. Those boys heired a ranch to take care of. Must be some reason for their bein' so far from home. If Dan Torkaway was runnin' an' if the other Torkaway was after him, that would get 'em away from home considerable, wouldn't it? Look. They waited a minute before shootin'. That shows they was surprised, both mebbe thinkin' Dan had made tracks a little faster than he had. But the other Torkaway wasn't too surprised not to have a smoke-wagon all cocked an' primed an' ready to his hand, though that ain't by no means the style, even in Tonca, not any more.

"One more thing I forgot to say. Dan Torkaway's brother took out after him that time, soon's he could get to his horse. Dan's horse is black, Squirty, real black."

Whack-Ear drew a long breath, exhausted.

"Mebbe some other reason . . . ," began Squirty.

"What kind o' reasons does a feller have to have to go gunnin' after his own brother year in, year out, while a ranch goes to work an' runs down on him?"

"Let's don't go jumpin' in the dark, Whack-Ear."

"Ain't any law case there, Squirty. But a fox sees more with his nose than you an' me read in the paper. All I says is . . . this feller ain't the kind of a feller I want singin' songs to Madge. An' any man with the blood of his pa on his hands an' his own brother gunnin' on his trail, he can't come in here an'. . . ."

"*Shush!* Listen!" commanded Squirty.

A man was walking toward the gate of the corral, whistling as he came. The dim starlight showed them a saddle on his hip. The two men against the fence by the gate fell silent, more because they had nothing public to talk about than because they wished to remain unobserved.

Thus, standing there in the shadows, they saw Dan Torkaway rope the big black, saddle, bridle over the hackamore, and tie the horse just outside the corral. After Torkaway had completed these operations, Squirty Wallace spoke, his voice pleasant and casual.

"Goin' some place?"

Dan Torkaway's unstartled acceptance of the question bespoke his previous knowledge that they were there. "Nope," he answered genially. "Just saddlin' my night horse. Kind o' like to keep him handy."

The two looked at each other in the dark.

He strolled beside them as they sauntered back toward the bunkhouse. Presently he spoke, volunteering speech for almost the first time since he had arrived at the Triangle R.

"Nice place here," he said. "I ain't never been much of a hand to settle in one place. Always hankered to ride on. But I think I'd sort of like to settle here for a while. If I was let."

They offered no answer to that.

"I ain't right sure," said Whiskers the following evening,

"that I done such a foxy thing when I started this Torkaway to singin' to Madge. Seemed to me like those hard-fried eyes o' his had a kind o' watery look when driftin' in her direction."

Whack-Ear slowly swung his shaggy head to look behind him. No one was near. "You jest played plain stupid, that's all you did!"

"Well, now," Whiskers rallied, seeing occasion for defense, "when I say he looked sloppy-eyed, I don't mean it in no unfittin' sense. He jest has a kind o' sad an' wistful look, that boy. But he's a good, clean lad, Whack-Ear. He can ride some an' keep his mouth shut purty fair. An' if he keeps a hoss ready an' saddled all night, I reckon we ain't much accustomed to makin' inquiries as to. . . ."

"She saddled up an' was for ridin' out with him this mornin'. An' I don't like it."

"But he didn't let her."

"That's somethin'. Shut up."

Squirty Wallace, Dixie Kane, and Dan Torkaway were coming around the corner of the bunkhouse.

"I see by the paper," said Squirty, "that some feller has worked out a plan whereby there's to be a redistribution o' wealth. It sure sounds good to me. I know positive that there's five fellers right here on this ranch that still has money, in spite o' them havin' been to town. It ain't fittin' or right. I recommends a game o' dealer's choice."

"There bein' only five of us back, I guess he means us," said Whack-Ear. "Did you hear, Whiskers? The boy wants to make a contribution to us!"

"I never was one to keep a young fellow down," admitted Whiskers. "Mebbe we should lighten his pockets, Whack-Ear, so's he can rise some."

"Leave me in out o' the cold," said Whack-Ear, leading the way into the dark bunkhouse.

A cold whisk of air was sliding down from the west, re-
minding them that the belated warm spell was probably to
end in a sudden burst of winter without further fooling.

"I smell snow!"

"See?" said Squirty, lighting a lamp. "Yesterday he figured it was summer. He wouldn't put paper in his bunk, not
him. Long toward mornin' I'll hear a kind o' frosty little voice
with icicles on it shiverin' in my ear . . . 'Squirty, I'm 'most
froze! Squirty, leave me crawl intuh your bunk! Squirty, I'm
like t'die! Squirty. . . .' Every little while from then on you
boys'll hear a loud *boomp!* That'll be nothin' but Whack-Ear
bein' moved out o' my bunk on to the floor again."

"Dixie," said Whack-Ear, hauling a homemade deal table
out into the middle of the room, "see how fast a good man can
get firewood into that stove."

"Who, me?" marveled the aggrieved bronco peeler. "I
brung in the last wood, an' I think. . . ."

"It wasn't by no means the last. We're gonna need wood
all winter," the straw boss corrected. "An' you stop that
thinkin' afore you bust somethin'. You hear?"

"I win the deal by common consent," said Whiskers,
waiving formalities. "Who wants some o' my poker insurance? For a certain price I guarantee to cover the insured
feller's losin's. See? By insurin' yourself with Mister Beck,
you can't do nothin' but win. We're playin' jest the usual six-
bit limit, ain't we? Who wants to feel safe?"

"How much does this here insurance cost?" Dan
Torkaway wanted to know.

"Depends on the feller," said Whiskers.

"How much for me?" asked Whack-Ear.

"Dollar 'n' a half, an' I pay back everythin' you lose."

"You're on!"

"All right, Whack-Ear. How about you, Squirty? For five

dollars, I insure you against an eight-dollar loss. Chance to make three dollars jest by sayin' the word."

"You go to hell!"

"I dunno about you, Torkaway," Whiskers continued, shuffling a crisp new deck. "Never seen you play. But fer four dollars I'll pay your losin's up to ten, seein's Squirty passed me up."

"Gosha'mighty," said Whack-Ear. "You figure we all gonna win?"

"Dixie Kane's here," Whiskers reminded him.

"Reckon I'll take the usual chance," Dan Torkaway decided.

"How much for me?" asked Dixie, coming away from the stove.

"Ten dollars covers a ten-dollar loss."

Dixie snorted. "You peetrified old hay rack," he commented, "I'll jest shake you down for that, come a middlin', decent hand."

Chips rattled out across the boards and were assembled into neat stacks. Cards flicked, spinning into five piles. Conversation subsided into sentences of one word each. Five faces became bleaker than a rawhide chip. The general redistribution of wealth had begun.

For two hours the men played by the light of the overhead lamps, while the cool breeze whoofed lightly against the closed door, and the fire clicked and sniffled in the potbellied stove. Contrary to tradition, Whack-Ear's pile dwindled to next to nothing and there stuck in a sulk, refusing alike to grow or give up the ghost. Squirty Wallace's elastic stack of chips rose and fell erratically. Prosperity swamped him with chips. A few hands later he had to buy more in order to play. Two big pots put him ahead of the game and two big mistakes reduced him to one white chip.

Likewise, contrary to tradition, Dixie Kane's pile steadily grew. The bronco peeler was in a run of luck that adapted itself perfectly to his unscientific but mystifying type of play. His three queens topped Whiskers's three jacks. His four aces beat Squirty's four kings. And with nothing in his hand but a king high, he bluffed Whack-Ear's flush into the discard. Whiskers was somewhat behind the game and Dan Torkaway was forging slowly ahead, seldom losing except to the confusing projects of Dixie Kane.

Whack-Ear, sitting with his back to the door, studied Dan Torkaway's face. Torkaway played with an air of abstraction, but without the peculiar blankness of countenance assumed by some of the other cowpunchers. Watching him, Whack-Ear noted irrelevantly that Torkaway's eyes were oddly deep and green—mild eyes that yet would be quick to see into the mind of a horse.

"Whiskers has the edge," said Squirty, as the ancient cowboy raked in a fair-size pot from him. "My honest, open face done that. Mebbe I could get by with murder, too, if I had a bunch o' brush hung in front o' my pan like him."

"Seems like I hear a horse out by the corral," said Dixie.

"A horse out by the corral," mocked Whack-Ear, dealing. "Now ain't that strange. Everybody in? Cards to gamblers."

"Guess I'll play these," said Dixie, passing the draw.

"One card," said Dan Torkaway, "will do me."

The others drew three each.

"Six-bits," said Dixie.

"Up the limit," said Torkaway.

"Ow," said Whiskers. "Signs tell grandpa to fold up his tent." He tossed away his cards.

"That knocks down my shingle," agreed Squirty, following Whiskers's example.

"Dealer out," said Whack-Ear. "Guess it's between you an' Torkaway, Dixie."

"Up six bits," said Dixie Kane.

"Up again," was Torkaway's reply.

Back and forth they raised. The pot increased to nine dollars, then twelve. The chips gave out, and the limit was thrown off by common consent. Torkaway bet thirty dollars; Dixie was forced to put up his saddle in order to raise. Torkaway was hard pressed to call, but he dug out fifty dollars more, his watch, an extra .45, a silk shirt. He was about to throw in his knife and buckskin gloves when Dixie stopped him.

"That's enough, mister," said Dixie. "You've matched my saddle all right."

"Then I raise you my bay horse," said Torkaway promptly. "Mind you, I say the bay."

Until now Dixie had remained calm and repressed, but now his excitement boiled over. "Good gosha'mighty!" he broke out. "What'll I raise at him?"

Whack-Ear, teetering on his soapbox seat, ran a huge hand through his shaggy hair and studied Dan Torkaway's face. He saw that same air of casual abstraction, in the eyes the same mild depths of green.

"How'll I raise him?" begged Dixie again, bobbing up and down on his seat. Dan Torkaway seemed to dream, his eyes resting sleepily on the door behind Whack-Ear's head.

A chill draft swept down the back of Whack-Ear's neck, and he knew the door had opened. He half moved to pivot on his box to kick the door shut, but the move checked itself, and Whack-Ear sat staring at Dan Torkaway's changing face. He saw Torkaway's green eyes wake and bore like steel into something in the door at his back, and, as he watched, gates closed behind those green eyes, so that they became peculiarly hard and shallow, as if backed by weathered limestone walls. The thin, curved scar, like an erased smile line, partly faded out against the changing color of Torkaway's face.

Whack-Ear turned and found, standing in the doorway, a man who looked peculiarly like Dan.

A pause, and then Whiskers's voice: "Shut that door."

The stranger kicked it shut without taking his eyes from Dan Torkaway's face.

"I'm raisin'," blurted Dixie Kane, "raisin' some way!" Dan Torkaway tossed away his cards in the gesture that admits defeat. They fell face up on the table. "My God," swore Dixie, "he had me beat!"

At this point even Dixie Kane became aware that another game was on than that of dealer's choice. A profound silence followed, in which they heard the wind and the soft explosion of an ember in the stove.

"Hod," said Dan Torkaway at last, and his voice trembled as he spoke, "I'm gonna have to shoot you yet."

"You seem surprised like," said the man that looked like Dan. "Didn't you know I was coming?"

"Yeah, I knew you'd come, Hod."

"Mebbe we should go outside."

"I reckon."

Slowly, as if with reluctance, Dan Torkaway rose from the deal table. The chips he left lay in a rambling, disorderly pile, like wreckage abandoned to the winds of chance. He walked to his bunk and drew from it a cartridge belt from which swung a holstered .45. His steady fingers moved deliberately as he strapped it on.

"Now jest a minute," said Whiskers Beck. "I don't want to seem like I'm buttin' into private affairs . . . an' this sure embarrasses me more'n it does you . . . but we don't have shootings at the Triangle R. Maybe we're kind of funny about that.

If some waddie wants to haul off an' bust somebody in the jaw in the excitement an' confusion of the moment, that's his look-out an' he takes his own risk. But a dee-liberate shooting is something else. We always take killin' rows to the Old Man, an', if he can't compromise it, why, the two boys are asked to take the fireworks somewhere else."

"Ain't a livin' man wouldn't say I had the right of it," said Hod after a moment. "I'm willin' to put my case up to anybody."

Dan Torkaway hesitated longer. "No one can settle this but jest us two, Hod. You know that," he said, and paused. "Still an' all, if you want to make a laughingstock out of yourself, it ain't nothin' to me. You're pushin' this business. I ain't."

"Laughingstock? We'll see who's a laughingstock," replied Hod in an ominous drawl. "Where's this Old Man of yours?"

"Step this way," said Whiskers. "You better come along, too, Whack-Ear."

Dan Torkaway went back to his bunk after a sheepskin jacket and his hat.

"Is it far?" Hod demanded.

"No," said Whiskers.

He led the way, Whack-Ear at his side. Hod and Dan Torkaway followed at a little distance.

"Where'd you get that stuff?" Whack-Ear demanded of Whiskers in a sidelong whisper. "I never heard o' no such rule around here. You talk like we lived in jest one continual revolution."

"I jest made it up out o' my head," Whiskers admitted. "If there's a murder lookin' for a place to happen, I don't figure to have it pick out here. Anyway, I like this Torkaway boy."

Left alone in the bunkhouse, Squirty Wallace and Dixie Kane stared at each other.

"I guess we ain't invited to this party," commented Squirty. "In fact, it's right plain that we ain't."

"He had me beat," marveled Dixie. "Beat easy. Say, what kind o' shindig we got here, anyhow?"

"Plenty," said Squirty. "I wouldn't sit in line with that window if I was you. Glass don't stop bullets very good. An' jest close the door, too, seein's you're up."

But outside, before Dixie had the door closed, they heard the sudden *chunk* of an impact, a strangling gasp for breath, and Whiskers's startled oath. Then Whack-Ear's voice, raised in a swift shout: "Squirty . . . Dixie, for God's sake, bring a light!"

Dixie rushed out, and Squirty, pausing to snatch down a lantern, followed closely on his heels. The windy night was darker than a wolf's den, and the dim, golden blur of the lantern was snuffed out by a fierce gust. They could see nothing.

"Here he is!" called Whiskers. "Gimme hand here!"

Dixie Kane, the youngest of them all, felt that swift, sickening sensation that can come over a man when someone is hurt, perhaps killed, in the mystery of the dark. He now made out the figures of Whiskers and Whack-Ear Banks, bending over a limp body on the ground. Hurrying forward, he helped carry it into the bunkhouse.

"It's Dan!" exclaimed Dixie.

Whiskers shook his head.

"Nope. T'other one." They laid the man on the nearest bunk.

"Is he knifed or jest whanged on the nut with an iron?" asked Squirty.

"Jest cracked with a fist," said Whiskers. "Jaw ain't

busted, either. Still works. He'll come out of it. Where's Dan?"

The wind slatted open the half-closed door, whisking cards from the table to the floor.

"Listen!" said Squirty, straightening up on his bowed legs.

The four stood in silence, looking at each other. Muffled, almost drowned in the voice of the wind, came the sound of running hoofs, a sound that diminished and died away.

The man that looked like Dan Torkaway stirred, twitched, and raised himself groggily upon one elbow. "Where is he?" he demanded thickly. "How'd I get in here?"

"He soaked you one," Whiskers volunteered. "You're comin' 'round all right, boy."

"Where is he?" demanded the stranger again.

"Gone," Whiskers told him. "Climbed on a hoss an' rode."

The prostrate man seemed to struggle to get this news through his head. Then suddenly he surged to his feet, and stood unsteadily.

"The damned coyote," he snarled. "Let me find my horse!" He started forward, swayed, and caught hold of Whiskers's arm. "Help me find my horse," he begged. "I gotta ride, mister. What'd I do with that horse?"

The others trooped after as Whiskers led him out.

Slowly but implacably the dim gray light of a cold and rimy dawn forced its way in through the smoky windows of the bunkhouse. It was a barren and unfriendly light, invading warm bunks to force a chill and unattractive reality into the place of pleasant dreams. At other seasons the cowpunchers might have rolled out in darkness in order to get breakfast over with in time to start work by the first light of day. But at this season there was no particular rush, and the daylight itself broke its own bad news.

Terrible Joe, the cook, had ridden in from Spring River at two in the morning, and he didn't feel very well. But he was dragged out of bed by his profession as inexorably as by a log chain. Heaving his bulging bulk out of his bunk, he pulled on boots and sobbed out the usual curses that were his morning ritual. Then he stumbled out in the direction of the mess shack.

Fifteen minutes later Squirty Wallace stirred uneasily and pulled his blankets over his head. A few minutes after that Whiskers Beck slowly pushed his shiny bald head out from under the covers, disentangled his beard from the blanket folds, and looked around.

"Whack-Ear! Hey, Whack-Ear!" he called, and a low moan answered from the opposite bunk. "Time to get the boys out, Whack-Ear!"

Whack-Ear slowly sat up and lowered stockinged feet to the floor. Whereupon Whiskers pulled the cover over his head again and went back to sleep. He had seen his duty and he had done it; that let him out. One by one they rolled out, following Whack-Ear's example—Squirty Wallace, Whiskers, and Dixie Kane. An ace of spades, face up on the floor, reminded Dixie of his winnings of the night before.

"Wonder where Torkaway is now?" he mused aloud.

At this a pile of blankets in a supposedly uninhabited bed squirmed slightly and came to life. Four cowpunchers stared a little blankly as a tousled head was thrust forth. It was Dan Torkaway.

The four Triangle R hands stared at each other as Torkaway piled himself out of his bunk and began to dress. Silently they pulled on overalls and boots; silently the five men filed out to the mess shack in response to Terrible Joe's horn.

Breakfast was a quiet meal. Not one question was asked by word or facial expression, or an explanation offered.

"Pass the 'taters," said Whiskers twice.

That was the full extent of the conversation.

After breakfast Whiskers found excuse to delay while Dixie, Squirty, and Whack-Ear proceeded to the corral to rope and saddle their ponies. As he had hoped, Dan Torkaway stopped him as he stepped out of the bunkhouse, his saddle on his hip.

"Whiskers," said Torkaway, "I'd like to talk to you some."

Whiskers Beck eased his saddle to the ground, and they stood together before the bunkhouse in the horizontal sunlight of the awakening day.

"I ain't stayin'," Torkaway went on. "I jest come back to get my war bag an' bed. But you been real white to me, Whiskers, you sure have. An' if that brother o' mine comes around here with a pack of lies, I want you should know the straight of it. So's, if anybody in particular should ever ask, you can tell 'em the truth."

"Sure, I'll tell her," said Whiskers.

Torkaway looked surprised, and the slender scar darkened a bit. But he went on.

"Here's the straight of how come I'm ridin' free an' loose, with Hod campin' on my trail. You remember a horse named Iron Paws, that crippled the boy at the Twin Peaks rodeo, four years back?"

"Heard of him. Killer, he was," Whiskers said.

"Yep. Iron Paws belonged to me an' pa. Then he got away. Three years back me an' Pa went horse huntin' an' found this Iron Paws keepin' together a herd of about twenty-five head. What with old Iron Paws punchin' 'em along behind an' a glass-eyed old pinto mare to lead, they were sure a spooky lot an' hard to catch. But we fooled 'em and headed 'em into a trap, a brush an' wire V with a corral at the point. Pa was hazin' 'em close. I was a little farther back. The herd went into the corral . . . all but Iron Paws. All of a sudden, as he saw he was tricked, Iron Paws went wild. He turned an' came chargin' back. 'Leave him go!' I yelled. But Iron Paws went straight for Pa. Killed him in the saddle, he did, before my eyes. You see, Pa's Forty-Five jammed. I tried to kill Iron Paws as he ran past. I emptied my gun at him, Whiskers. But the Torkaways jest ain't good shots. He got away."

Torkaway paused, and rolled a cigarette. "Hod an' I rode out after that, aimin' to ride down Iron Paws an' make him coyote meat. But we disagreed as to where he was, third day out. Hod had to look where he knew any reasonable horse would go. But I knew Iron Paws. I went where no reasonable horse would go. An' there he was." Torkaway paused again, inhaled deeply, and blew the smoke out through his nose. "I killed Iron Paws, Whiskers." The gray stone gates closed behind the green eyes, in a way that somehow made Torkaway's whole face a mask. "I killed him. You gotta take my word for that. You gotta believe I killed him because I say so!"

"Ain't doubtin', am I?" said Whiskers.

"Ridin' back was about a six days' ride, by then. Right after killin' Iron Paws, I got a big shock. Not more'n a mile away I come on somethin' so strange I could hardly believe my own eyes. There was another Iron Paws, jest a livin', spittin' image o' the first. 'Course, I thought right away Iron Paws wasn't dead or I was crazy or somethin'. I took out after this horse. Pretty soon I saw that this one's kind o' tame-like. Different from Iron Paws, thataway. I whistled at him, like I always whistle at a horse. Whiskers, he stopped!"

"Terlegaphy," said Whiskers Beck.

"What?"

"Nothin'. Go on."

"I got down, an' he let me walk near. I roped him. He led easy. He even let me look in his mouth. Iron Paws was nearly ten years old, Whiskers, though they looked so much alike, both black without marks, an' with those blue-glass eyes. When I went back to look, Iron Paws still lay dead. Next day my horse broke his leg in a badger hole. Rather than walk back, of course, I took a chance on losin' my saddle an' broke this new horse. He sure fought. But I rode him in. Whiskers, there ain't but one explanation. This horse that I got here looks so much like Iron Paws, he sure must be Iron Paws' colt!"

"Seems likely," Whiskers agreed.

"But Hod wouldn't listen. He swore it was Iron Paws, an' thinks so yet."

"Didja let him look in the mouth?" Whiskers asked.

The limestone walls were hard behind Torkaway's eyes. "A man has got to take my word, when I give it," he said. "I wouldn't let him hog-tie my horse."

"Hog-tie?"

"Jest because I can put my hand in this horse's mouth don't mean anybody can," Torkaway explained, "not with the horse on his feet."

"Oh," said Whiskers, pulling at his white mustache.

"Hod was bound he was goin' to kill Iron Paws' colt. So I rode off in a spatterin' of poorly aimed lead, leavin' my half of the ranch we inherited to him. But Hod is real obstinate. I've kept ridin' an' Hod's kept follerin' on. Twice he's caught up . . . once in Tonca, once in Coulter's Pass. Both times he fired on the black horse at sight. I think a sight of that black, Whiskers. Never was such a horse if handled right. An' not a speck of bad in him no place. Whiskers, there ain't any bad in Iron Paws' colt, not when he's treated right. But Hod swears he'll never quit until my black horse is dead. Seems like when a

62

man's own brother takes after him, there ain't nothin' will stop him, never."

"Yep, nobody comes unlicked any faster than a brother," Whiskers admitted.

"I jest wanted you to know it ain't my fault I got this bother, Whiskers," said Torkaway. The gates opened behind the green eyes so that they became deep and full of appeal. "I ain't dealt to no one off the bottom of the deck, an' I wanted you to know I stand square in case anyone should ask."

Abruptly Torkaway turned away and strode toward the corral. Whiskers did not proceed to saddle at once, but rolled himself a cigarette, and sat down on the bench by the door to ponder the odd yarn that he had heard. Presently Torkaway reappeared, leading the big black, saddled.

"I gotta tie on my things," he said.

"I'll hold your hoss," Whiskers offered.

"I . . . I dunno but what he's better tied," Torkaway said. "Never was much to stand."

He tied the black at a nearby rail. Whiskers sat gazing at the stallion, marveling at the animal's muscled beauty. He, at least, could understand why a man might go riding on indefinitely if it was for the sake of a horse like that.

Torkaway came out of the bunkhouse, and began strapping his bedroll to the saddle of the black.

"Kane's winnings are in his bunk," he said.

Whiskers nodded.

"Well," said Torkaway, "good bye."

"So long," said Whiskers.

Through the cottonwoods and around the corner of the bunkhouse came a foaming gray horse at a dead gallop. His shoulders, black with sweat, flashed in the sun as he pulled up on his haunches. Lather like shaving soap dripped from under the saddle blanket. Out of the gray's saddle dropped the man that looked like Dan.

The newcomer gave his brother hardly more than a glance. His eyes were on the tethered black, the horse that Dan Torkaway claimed was Iron Paws' colt. Deliberately he drew his gun, deliberately he aimed.

Torkaway flung himself through the air at the man with the gun. They went down together, the gun discharging in the air. When they came up, Dan Torkaway was in possession of his brother's gun.

"You son-of-a-bitch," swore the other, "put down that iron and fight!"

"Hod," begged Dan, "for God's sake, pull up. It ain't the horse, I tell you. It ain't Iron Paws, Hod!"

"You're shieldin' the horse that killed Pa," said Hod, his voice grating and low. "An' I'm goin' to kill that horse, the murderin' bastard, even if I have to kill you!"

"I swear to high heaven, Hod, that horse ain't him!"

Only the vaguest suggestion of an obstinate uncertainty showed in Hod's face as he replied. "Then you let me look in his mouth!"

"No," said Dan. "I'd see you in hell first!"

"I got a right to look him in the mouth," persisted Hod, "an' I'm gonna!"

He stepped toward the black.

"Hod," said Dan, his voice like steel, "I'll shoot you down the second you touch that horse!"

"Then shoot, you son-of-a-bitch!"

"I'm tellin' you . . . !" shouted Dan, raising the gun.

Whiskers, stepping up behind Dan, snatched down his gun arm and held it with his full weight.

"For God's sake, Hod," yelled Dan, "look out!"

Quietly Hod approached the horse, speaking gently.

Slowly he raised a hand to grasp a silken black ear. His hand touched it.

Something exploded within the black hide at the touch of the man's hand. The stallion reared backward as if cut with a whip, squealing in a vicious rage. The hackamore snapped like paper. Wild-eyed, screaming, with ears flattened and mouth wide, the black plunged at the man, striking with driving forehoofs. Hod dropped and rolled, and the horse went over. The crazy beast whirled as if in mid-air, sprang to trample with four hoofs at once.

Dan Torkaway wrenched his gun arm loose from Whiskers's relaxed grasp. As he fired, the black came down in a heap, apparently on Hod's prostrate body. The black struggled to rise, got to his knees. Dan fired again, and the black head sank a little. Again—again.

"Good God!" burst out Whiskers, clawing frantically for the place his own gun might have been. "He's jest cutting him to pieces any old way!"

The Torkaway boys were not good shots. The black rolled over on his side, trembled, and was still.

Whack-Ear Banks and Dixie Kane had sprinted up and were dragging Hod Torkaway from under the body of the black. Squirty Wallace came racing on his buckskin, dropped from the saddle without stopping the horse, and sprang to help them. The three carried the battered man into the bunkhouse, where they laid him on the same bunk that had received him the night before.

Whiskers Beck, following them in, turned at the door to look at Dan Torkaway. Dan had sat down shakily on the bench by the door, his face an oyster gray, his hands dropped limply between his knees. His gun had fallen to the ground. He had eyes only for the red-stained carcass that had been his horse.

"You seem to be comin' 'round all right," said Whiskers presently to the man in the bunk. "Barrin' them fingers, you ain't much more'n shook up. You don't seem lucky, boy. Seems like every time we see you we start carryin' you in."

"Listen," said Hod Torkaway, and Whiskers noted again how much the man looked like Dan. "Is that . . . killer dead?"

"Plenty," said Whiskers. "Plumb weighted down with lead."

Hod Torkaway seemed to breathe more easily.

"Listen. Dan won't talk to me. That boy's got an obstinate streak, some way. You got any influence with him?"

"Not much," said Whiskers. "But as much as anybody here, I reckon."

"Tell him, if Iron Paws is dead, we're all square. Tell him I even admit that horse wasn't Iron Paws at all. I won't even look in his mouth to see, now he's dead. You tell Dan I want he should come back an' work our cattle with me, an' we'll say no more of it."

"He's fixin' to ride," said Whiskers, "but I'll go try."

Outside, Dan Torkaway had transferred the savings of a lifetime, consisting of saddle, bedroll, and war bag to the back of the horse with the whiskered jaw.

"Dixie wouldn't take the bay," he told Whiskers ruefully. "He said he hadn't covered that bet, though he was goin' to raise. He was for callin' all bets off, seein' I had him beat when I dropped, an' us not comin' to a showdown for special reasons, and so on. But I made him keep the rest of the stuff. Well, leastwise, I'm able to ride, Whiskers."

He forced a shadow of a smile.

"Hod was sayin' how he thought. . . ."

"I know, Whiskers. Tell Hod I got nothin' against him. I'll

ride around and see him someday. Glad to know he ain't
hurt. Don't want to talk to him now, though, Whiskers."

"You ain't goin' back to your ranch in Arizona?"

"Reckon not, Whiskers. Aim to ride a while."

"There's some wouldn't mind seein' you stay right on
here, Torkaway."

"I thought of that . . . stayin' here, I mean, if I was let. Had
time to do a pile of thinkin', ridin' out last night like I did. But
somehow, one kind of calls for the other . . . stayin' here an'
goin' back, don't you see? An' the two don't hook up, either."
Whiskers didn't see, but he said nothing. "So I guess I'll jest
keep on."

"Keep on what?"

"Ridin', Whiskers, ridin' on. Got the habit now, I guess.
Well, good bye, Whiskers."

"Wait, now, Torkaway. You're shook up like. Wait a
while, an'. . . ."

To Torkaway came the feeling that he had talked until he
had made a fool of himself. He forced himself to grin apologetically, then touched his horse with a spur. The whiskered
bay moved off at a fox-trot.

As Torkaway disappeared beyond the cottonwoods, Whiskers turned with sudden resolution to the carcass of the black
horse.

"There's somethin' I gotta see," he said to himself.

He stooped by the motionless head and his hands took
hold of the velvety nose and jaw in the position of a man
about to open a horse's mouth. Then suddenly he stood up.

"Nope," said he. "Iron Paws or Iron Paws' colt, it ain't
any business of mine. I ain't goin' to look-see. An' neither is
anybody else without considerably squelchin' this committee
o' one. I can be real obstinate, too, when I've a mind."

For a long moment he stared after Torkaway, now a tiny,

receding figure on the valley trail. Whiskers scratched his head as he stared pondering several things.

"Strange fellers," he said at last, as he turned away. "Strange fellers, the both."

Gunnies from Gehenna

Old Sam Proctor pulled a smoking branding iron from the fire and slapped it on the shoulder of a calf that was being held down by a tall, gray-haired cattleman. He turned his head away and half closed his eyes.

"Seems like I ain't got the heart to do it any more, Nevada," he complained dolefully as the abused calf sprang up and went bawling to its mother. "When I was a young scamp, I didn't give a damn. I branded thousands of 'em. But now it seems to hurt me more'n it does them."

"Yeah," growled Nevada Morrison skeptically, "that's what Dave Ormsby said when he shot Bull Harris through the gizzard. Any time you think it's hurtin' you more'n it does the calf, Sam, I'll hold this hot brandin' iron on the seat o' your pants, an' see how quick you change your mind. You're gettin' too damned sympathetic since that Gospel sharp talked you into gittin' religion."

Sam mopped his streaming brow with a red bandanna, and looked out over the smoky prairie. He could see miles of the thread of a trail, shimmering in the heat from the top of the hill where they were working. Solemnly taking in the vast panorama, Sam pulled a plug of tobacco from his pocket and bit off an enormous chew.

"Some *hombre* is comin' like Gehenna," he said after a pause.

Nevada grinned, and looped his rope preparatory to dragging in another calf.

"Somebody's after him," Sam went on. "He's sure burnin' up hossflesh, Nevada. That's the trouble with these crazy rannies nowadays. They ain't got no regard for a dumb critter. Now when I was young. . . ."

"Yeah." Nevada interrupted with a grin. "I remember how you used to go to town on that little buckskin. Every time you got forty dollars in your jeans, you went that twelve miles like a shot out o'. . . ."

"Gehenna," interposed Sam. "Gehenna, Nevada. It don't sound so much like cussin'."

For some time Sam stood on the rocky promontory that dropped straight to the trail. The hill sloped gradually behind him. He could see the fugitive coming steadily forward, his horse with head down, running with the heartless, dragging gait that, even at that distance, showed utter exhaustion. Far behind, yet gaining noticeably, were five riders.

Nevada strode up and stood beside his friend.

"Five on to one," growled Sam. "It ain't fair."

"Mebbe he's one o' them bandits that stuck up the stage last week," countered Nevada.

"I don't give a hang," Sam insisted. "It ain't fair. It's a heck of a sheriff we got, Nevada, when he has to call out a whole danged posse to run down one man."

"He must be a bad one. Mebbe he held up the bank."

"I don't care a dang if he did," Sam fired up. "They ain't got no business to jump on him like that. Five on to one! An' then they'll prob'ly take the poor fellah an' put him in the pen. Or they might even string him up without a trial. Sech things has been done in this here country, Nevada."

Sam puckered his lips to discharge an overload of tobacco juice.

The fugitive reached the bottom of the hill. Suddenly his horse stumbled and fell. The man squirmed out of the saddle and rose unsteadily to his feet.

Sam glanced back at the mounts of Nevada and himself,

and at the extra horse that carried firewood and grub on the ride over the ranch to pick up calves that had escaped the spring roundup.

"This way!" he shouted to the man. "Come up here, ol'-timer, an' we'll see you out o' this."

"Now what the devil . . . ?" began Nevada, staring at his friend.

"Gehenna, Nevada. Gehenna. It don't never pay to use cuss words unless it's absolutely necessary. We're goin' to help that poor fellah out o' his misery an' tribulations. Five on to one is too danged many."

The man came climbing toward them up the steep side of the hill. Nevada looked at the swarthy face, the heavy, black mustache, the unshaven chin, and the close-set, small eyes. He shook his head.

"He looks like a murderer," he suggested in a low voice.

"It don't make no difference if he is," Sam retorted. "There's good in every danged *hombre* on the whole danged earth, if you can jest find it. You should always help a poor creature in distress, Nevada, even if he is runnin' away from the sheriff. You never know when he'll turn right around an' help you do the same, for a good deed ain't never forgot."

The man came puffing up the hill.

"Gents," he began. "Gents, I never done it. I. . . ."

"It's all right, stranger," Sam interrupted. "We got a extra horse here, and it won't be shakes till we get away from that imitation sheriff with his tin badge an' his army."

Grumbling under his breath, Nevada followed the other two. The fugitive, nervously glancing behind, sprang into the saddle and rode ahead down the green slope.

"He's a bad looker, Sam," whispered Nevada. "If he lives by the sword, he'll perish by the sword. 'Vengeance is mine says the Lord.' "

He glanced backward as the sheriff and his posse reached the top of the hill. They pulled up their lathering, blowing horses and looked at the escaping fugitive. The man snarled back at them, disclosing huge, yellow teeth. Then he turned deliberately and rode straight for the trail that he had abandoned when his horse fell. With a shout the posse rode down the slope to cut him off.

"You damned fool!" ejaculated Nevada. "Where the hell do you think you're goin'?"

With a snarl, the man turned. His hand swept down to his thigh, and he snapped a .45 from the holster.

"I'm goin' where I please," he cried, "an' you two ol' fossils is goin' with me. I need you."

With his free hand he lashed Sam's horse with a quirt, and then struck Nevada's mount across the flank. He drove his spurs home, and the three went dashing toward the trail that wound like a gray thread across the prairie.

The fugitive rode closely behind Sam and Nevada, cursing and striking at the horses that were straining every muscle under the lash and spur. A bullet whined close to them as the posse came within rifle range.

"You shore got us in bad with John Law, Sam," complained Nevada as he lay closely to his horse's back. "This feller is a killer."

"There's always a chance for the wicked to see the error of their ways, Nevada," Sam replied serenely. "If a man whacks you on one cheek, you should always turn the other. You know, Nevada, we ain't been chased by a sheriff for a heck of a while. Sorta makes a feller feel young again, don't it?"

Again came the snarl of a bullet. The posse was gaining. Nevada set his lips grimly as the quirt descended on the rump of his horse, and the tortured brute dashed forward with every ounce of strength. The man they had tried to save was shouting curses at them.

Puffs of smoke spurted out from gun barrels, and hot bullets hummed past like angry bees. They could hear the sheriff's voice as he commanded them to stop, but they held straight on toward the trail, the three horses at a dead run.

The dusty trail loomed ahead. A moment later they turned into it with Nevada wondering what power had protected them from the fusillade of bullets that snarled about them. Once Nevada glanced at the grim face of the man who drove them on. His yellow teeth were bared in a snarl, and his gun was held straight on the two men who had befriended him.

"A killer," Nevada muttered. "I wonder what this ol' rooster of a Sam is goin' to get us into next."

Sam acted as though he was enjoying the discomfiture of the sheriff.

"Five on to one!" he cried once, ignoring the fact that he was being menaced by the end of a gun. "We shore need a new sheriff, Nevada. They must o' shot twenty times at us an' never burnt a feather. Mebbe we'll reform this here ranny before we're done with him."

"Reform, hell!" ejaculated Nevada as he again glanced at the grim, relentless face.

"Say Gehenna, Nevada. It don't sound so much like cussin'."

Slowly they drew ahead. Then the sheriff and his posse drew up their horses and slowed to a walk. Presently they were no more than dots on the horizon.

"Turn here," the dark-faced man ordered, "an' head for them cottonwoods over there by the pond."

Without a word Sam and Nevada rode toward the grove. Apparently their fast journey was coming to an end.

The neighing of a horse sounded from the deep shade of

the trees as they approached. Sam's mount threw up its head and answered.

Three men strode out into the sunlight, and stood watching the little group as it approached.

"It looks as though the hangman has been missin' something for a long time," muttered Nevada as he eyed the three narrowly.

"What you got, Gyp?" called one of them. He was wearing a dirty pair of Angora chaps. "You bringin' in more recruits for the gang, or did you pick up a couple o' Egyptian mummies on the range?"

"You're shore pickin' 'em young an' handsome now, ain't you, Gyp?" said another.

"Gyp an' his gang o' ramblin' young rannies," called the third, a tarnished range dude.

The man they called Gyp rode behind Sam and Nevada without answering.

"Sam," gasped Nevada under his breath, "this here must be that Gypsy Ludlow, the hoss thief from over the divide. He's been raisin' hell over in Critchew County."

"Gehenna, Nevada," interposed Sam mildly.

"Well, I've heard some goshawful wicked stories about what him an' his gang has been pullin' off."

Sam did not answer. His lithe, wiry form was straight in the saddle, and he smiled at the three men who had ambled out of the grove.

They drew up at the command of the swarthy man who had herded them there, and then went forward among the trees to a campfire. A slaughtered yearling lay nearby, and steaks were broiling over the fire on forked sticks.

"Git down!" Gyp ordered. The two old men slipped out of the saddle. "Take their guns," the outlaw went on. "We're gettin' out o' here *pronto*, 'cause there's a damned sheriff on our trail with four men. We'll leave these two ol' buzzards here, but we're takin' their hosses. Never pass up a good hoss. That's my motto, 'cause if you don't want him yourself, you can always find somebody what does.''

Nevada glanced at Sam who stood staring at Gypsy Ludlow as though he could not believe what he had heard.

The guns of the two cattlemen were jerked from the holsters, and they stood helplessly as the gang broke camp.

"Watch them ol' *hombres,* Dave," ordered Gypsy Ludlow as he took up a piece of beef that was broiling over the coals, and bit huge chunks from it with his yellow teeth.

Sam and Nevada remained close to the horses. Dave looked at them with a grin on his twisted face. Sam decided that he didn't like that face. It was the sneering, defiant face of a man that was born to hang.

The old cattleman passed his hand over his brow, and leaned weakly against the saddle. If Dave had not been so contemptuous of the two old men, he might have noticed that Sam's hand was against the rope snapped in its loop by the saddle horn, and that his fingers were moving slowly.

The other two men were packing blankets and meat in the saddlebags. Gypsy Ludlow went on bolting his meal.

Sam glanced at Nevada and made a slight motion with his head. Nevada answered with a wink.

"I was in town lookin' over a bunch o' Six-G hosses in a big corral," Gypsy Ludlow was complaining, "when a waddy that knew me over at Sattler recognized me. He set up a holler an' I had to grab the first hoss I saw to get away. It must have gone a long ways today, 'cause it played out before I'd gone ten miles. It would have been a cinch to get them hosses if that coyote hadn't recognized me. They was worth at least four thousand dollars, too."

"It's a danged shame, Gyp." The guard grinned. "We all

know you'd rather steal hosses than eat. Can't we go back to-night?"

"Not with that posse lookin' for us." Gypsy Ludlow poured a tin cup half full of black coffee and sipped it noisily. "We'll come back for 'em someday, and we'll come a-shootin'. They can't run me out o' town thataway an' not get hurt up some."

Sam's face was very stern. He glanced at Nevada, and nodded.

With a yell Nevada jumped right at the guard. His long legs flew out and caught the man fully in the stomach. The two went down together with Nevada on top. Punching and kicking, they rolled over and over.

The other bandits spun around, and the dude reached for his gun. A rope whirred through the air, settled over his head, and he was yanked off his feet.

"*Gawk!*" he howled as he hit the ground with the rope around his neck.

The gun flew from his hand and fell near Sam.

The old cattleman sprang forward and gathered up the fallen weapon as a bullet spanged into the ground. It had gone within an inch of his head.

"*Ye-e-e-ow!*" howled Nevada as he brought down his fist against the chin of the guard. The man's head snapped back and he sank down very limply.

Gypsy Ludlow had stood with drawn weapon as the two were rolling over and over. Now he threw it down on Nevada.

Spang!

The gun flew from Gypsy Ludlow's hand, and a red groove appeared across his wrist. Sam had shot from the ground.

Nevada yanked the guard's weapon from its holster, and fired it twice at the fourth man who had suddenly come into the fray. His arm fell limply at his side, and he stood looking foolishly at the tall cattleman.

The whole affair had not taken more than ten seconds. One of the men was unconscious. Another had a smashed arm. Another was prone on the ground, and the leader, Gypsy Ludlow, was disarmed and helpless.

The outlaw chief stood glaring at the two old men. His dark face was aflame with rage. His lips were drawn back in a snarl that disclosed the huge, yellow teeth.

Sam mopped his brow and looked about him. "Not bad for a couple of old cowpokes like us, Nevada," he remarked. "You old fire-eater, you knocked out that *hombre* jest like you cleaned up on Rat Newbury when we was young hellikers workin' for the Circle B."

"Yeah," retorted Nevada sourly, "he made me mad."

"I'll see you roastin' in hell before we're through with this," Gypsy Ludlow raged.

"Gehenna, friend," Sam corrected. "It don't sound so much like cussin'."

Then Gypsy Ludlow showed that his reputation as a horse thief and outlaw was not founded on bluff. A sudden leap took him to the back of Sam's horse. Viciously he sank his spurs into the animal's sides. There was a frantic drumming of hoofs, and he went dodging between the trees toward the prairie.

Nevada's gun barked, and the bullet tore a strip of bark from a tree within a foot of the outlaw's head.

"Don't shoot!" cried Sam. "You might hit Baldy."

Baldy was his favorite horse.

He swung into Nevada's saddle and went dashing after the retreating Gypsy Ludlow.

"Take care o' them three bad *hombres,* Nevada!" he shouted.

The tall cattleman held his gun on the three. Two of them were on their feet and the other was sitting up.

"Line up, you dirty horse thieves," he commanded. "The first one that makes an off move is gonna eat lead."

He stood them with backs toward him, and waited for Sam.

"You're bleedin' like a stuck hawg," he remarked presently to the man he had shot through the arm. "You can tie up your hurt, but don't make no false motions."

Gypsy Ludlow dashed straight for the green prairie. Sam came out of the trees 200 yards behind.

Far to the left five dots moved slowly against the horizon. Gypsy Ludlow saw them, and turned so they were directly in the rear. He dug his spurs into the red flanks of the horse, and roared a profane challenge as he sped over the prairie.

The bare, yellow spots that showed a prairie-dog town caused Sam to slow down and ride carefully. Gypsy Ludlow widened the gap between them, for he dashed forward at full speed.

Slowly Sam gained, and the gap closed. Gypsy Ludlow turned from time to time, shook his fist, and howled curses at the pursuing cattleman. Evidently the outlaw did not have a concealed gun, and Sam's rifle was not in the saddle boot.

Twice Sam threw down the revolver and aimed at the retreating outlaw. Then he shook his head and put the gun back into its holster. He could not bring himself to shoot an unarmed man.

With a vicious yank at the reins, Gypsy Ludlow pulled up Baldy who came to a stop in four or five stiff-legged jumps. Then he turned and rode straight at Sam, his dark face flaming with wrath.

Sam whipped out the gun and held it steadily on the

outlaw. Gypsy Ludlow rose high in the stirrups and left the saddle in a leap straight at Sam. The two fell from the horse and rolled on the grass.

Sam coiled up as a spring, and shot out his boots straight to the chest of the outlaw. Gypsy Ludlow gave a howl.

Sam was all whalebone and rawhide. His fist shot out, and Gypsy Ludlow's head snapped back. Blood dripped from the outlaw's clenched lips. His huge arms swept around Sam, but the old cattleman wriggled free.

Still on his knees, Gypsy Ludlow jerked forward and grasped Sam around the thighs. In vain the cattleman struck down. Gypsy Ludlow, his face protected and his head as hard as boiler iron, bored in, gripping tighter and tighter in his effort to throw Sam to the earth. His hand reached up, and he pulled the gun from the cattleman's holster.

Sam grasped the huge wrist with his right hand as his left fist smashed into the dark face. Gypsy Ludlow loosed his hold, as blood spouted from his nose.

With a triumphant cry, he drew down the gun on the old man. Then he catapulted to the ground as Sam's boot caught him fairly on the jaw.

The fight was over. The old cattleman rubbed his stomach and made a wry face. He was not injured, but he had swallowed his chew of tobacco in the excitement.

A few minutes later Sam approached the grove. He was leading Nevada's horse with the battered, bound Gypsy Ludlow.

Five men were galloping up on tired, sweating horses.

"Here's your man, Sheriff!" Sam called as they approached. "It's about time you was gettin' around."

Nevada grinned. "So you got him, did you, Sam?" he gloated.

"Got him! Of course, I got him. Did you think I wasn't man enough to do it?"

"I knowed you was man enough to get him," soothed Nevada, "but I thought mebbe you was so damned sympathetic, you'd let him go. You should love your enemies, Sam. That's what you've been tellin' me."

"This here is different," Sam flared. "This skunk wasn't no stage bandit or bank robber or even a plain murderer. He was a hoss thief. Think of it, Nevada! A hoss thief! An' you, you dog-goned ol' gunny from Gehenna, you was helpin' him get away."

Hard-Boiled

Old Sam Proctor and his bosom friend, Nevada Morrison, were sitting in front of the general store in Elk City. The sun had gone down in a blaze of glory, and a full moon was pushing itself above the haze in the east, looking abnormally huge and red in the refracted light.

A group of small boys came charging up the street, pulling a ramshackle wagon. They dropped the tongue as they passed and scooted away. The wagon careened to the side of the street and came to a stop against a hitch rack within a few feet of Sam and Nevada.

Neither of the old men made any comment, for it was Halloween, and comment was unnecessary.

"This sure is one topsy-turvy ol' world," Sam opined moodily, as he rocked back and forth holding one knee in his clasped hands. "I dunno what's comin' over people nowadays. It seems all they give a dang hoot about is makin' whoop jamboree."

"Yeah, I suppose that's right, Sam," drawled Nevada sleepily. "Yeah, I reckon there's been a big change since me and you was young."

He took off his big hat and shook the heavy mane of iron-gray hair that adorned his head.

"Whatever you want to happen never happens," went on Sam dolefully. "Everything you set your heart on always comes out the other way. Seems like only one thing is sure, an' that is we're all gettin' nearer the grave every day. Some place a grave is waitin' for us, prob'ly all green an' pretty-like, an' we can't get away from it. It's a-sayin' . . . 'Come on,

81

Nevada. Come on, Sam. I'm a-waitin' for you, an' soon there won't be nothin' left o' you but a couple o' skulls an' a mess o' dry bones.' There ain't nothing we can do about it 'cause. . . ."

Nevada turned and stared at his friend with wide eyes and open mouth. "Say!" he ejaculated. "What in thunder is eatin' you, Sam? Carryin' on about graves an' skulls an' bones thataway! You give a feller the creeps. What's on your mind, Sam? Somethin' seems to be worryin' you."

"Oh, it ain't nothin' special, Nevada, but it kinda makes a feller think when he sees this young crowd that's goin' to carry things on when we're gone. It's jest like seein' a bunch of woollies comin' into a cattle range."

Nevada grunted, crossed his long legs, and folded his hands over his knees. He looked at the moon and whistled "The Cowboy's Lament".

A wild yell broke the stillness of the autumn night. Four men dashed into town in a cloud of dust. Their six-shooters roared out again and again, and then tongues of flame licked the twilight as they fired into the air.

Both Sam and Nevada sprang to their feet.

"What's goin' on around here?" Nevada growled. "This ain't no roundup. This here is a peaceful community. Them fellers ought to be run in for actin' thataway. If I didn't know that Snake Simmons's gang o' rustlers from Buck Creek was all in jail, I'd say it was them."

Sam's name was whispered softly, and he looked up to see a woman peering out of the doorway. He recognized her as a mixed-blood squaw from Buck Creek, and he went into the store to hear what she had to say.

In a few moments he returned.

"Nevada," he growled, "Gehenna is poppin'!"

"No," Nevada drawled, "it ain't nothin' but four fool cowpokes tryin' to show off how tough they think they are."

"Listen, Nevada! Winona Peters rode clear over here from Buck Creek to tip us off. Snake Simmons an' his gang has got out on bail, an' they've come over here to kill Sheriff Burton."

"What!" shouted Nevada.

"That's what. Winona found it out somehow. You know Burton got the evidence on Snake an' his gang an' he's goin' to send 'em all to the pen. Now if they can bump him off, nobody can testify against 'em, an' they'll all get off slicker'n grease. They're goin' to start raisin' whoop jamboree around town till Burton interferes. Then they're goin' to stage a fake fight an' Burton will be bumped off accidental-like an' nobody will know who done it."

Nevada scratched his gray head. "Yeah," he drawled, "an' they might get away with it at that. Sam, we've got to go an' warn Burton as to what's up. He's only been out o' bed three or four days from the way he got shot up in that ruckus with Snake's gang."

"Mebbe so, but that won't make no difference to him. He'd tackle Snake an' the whole danged town of Buck Creek if he had to be wheeled out in a chair."

The two men strode up the street to the small building that served as sheriff's office and jail.

Burton was putting on his hat when they entered. He was a young man, smooth-shaven and serious of face. They noticed that his hands trembled as he buckled on a huge belt with holster swung low on the left side, and they knew the trembling was from weakness and not from fear.

" 'Evenin', Sheriff," greeted Nevada with outstretched hand. "We come in for a little gab-fest. Take off your hat an' set."

"Sorry," answered Burton. "Make yourselves at home a

few minutes till I come back. There's a lot o' hilarity goin' on that I've got to stop. I don't object to a little fun on Halloween, but this is goin' too danged far."

"Son," asked Nevada mildly, "do you know who's doin' that shootin'?"

"No, but I'll soon find out."

In a few words Nevada told the young sheriff of the plot against his life. "Now," he continued, "the way to handle this is jest to set down an' do nothin'. Them rannies ain't goin' to do no damage unless you show up an' try to stop 'em. They'll blow off a little, an' tomorrow you can have warrants issued to arrest 'em if they come back. Now set down, son, an' me an' Sam will tell you some stories about how we done up the Bridleton gang thirty years ago."

Burton shook his head, and pulled his hat low down above his eyes.

"Now, looky here, Burton," Sam cried, "you gotta use your head in a case like this! There ain't no sense in goin' out to round up that gang. They're here to get you, an' nobody but a young jackass would play into their hands the way you're doin'. You ain't in no condition even to be out o' bed, to say nothin' o' havin' a gunfight with the toughest bunch o' rannies in the county."

"No!" answered Burton grimly. "It's up to me to keep order in this town. If I can't do it, I may as well be under ground."

"You stubborn young mule!" cried Nevada. "You can't fight that bunch. You're crazy to try it. You need depitties to turn a trick like that."

Burton turned with a grin on his white face.

"All right, you two ol' rannies, I'll deputize you both. Here's your stars."

He reached in his desk, and then pinned a star on Nevada's shirt front, and one on the lapel of Sam's leather coat.

"Well, I'll be damned!" exclaimed Nevada. "Sam, we're shore-enough depitties."

"Huh," Sam grunted, "what are we supposed to do?"

"You are deputized to keep law an' order in Elk City," returned the still grinning Burton. "An' since you're so concerned in the matter, you can look out for the sheriff an' see that he's kept safe for further service."

Sam pulled off his big hat and flung it violently on the floor.

"All right, son!" he cried. "We'll do it. We'll mix it with that bunch till they wish they was back in jail where it's peaceful an' safe. But you gotta stay out o' the way where you won't get hurt." He sprang forward and threw both arms around Burton, pinning the sheriff's arms to his sides.

"Git his danged guns, Nevada," he gasped.

Burton was taken completely off guard. He tried to break away from Sam, but Nevada's powerful grip closed on his neck, and his gun was jerked from the holster.

"Into a cell with him," panted Sam.

They hustled the sheriff through the little hall to the cells that were open. In another moment Burton was confined behind bars, and the key was in Sam's pocket.

"You're under arrest!" he shouted. "I hereby arrest both o' you ol' fossils, an' I tell you it will go hard with you if you don't unlock this door."

"Now, son," soothed Sam, "don't take on thataway. A good boss knows how to make his men do all the work, so jest sit back an' think about your sins, an' leave it all to your depitties. I wouldn't say nothin' if you was able to get around, but now you gotta stay in that jail till them hard *hombres* has left town."

The two old men put out the lights, went out, and locked

the office door, with the raging sheriff locked safely in his own jail.

"Listen to him cuss." Nevada grinned as they paused near the door. "He don't even know how to cuss good, let alone shootin' it out with Snake."

Sam was examining his cedar-handled .45 in the faint light.

"Sometimes I begin to think I ain't as good with a gun as I used to be, Nevada," he said. "Do you remember the time I shot all the buttons off Dude Hillaker's pants over at the Cheyenne rodeo?"

A burst of shooting came from the saloon a block away.

"There they go!" cried Nevada. "They're shootin' up the place."

It was early evening. The streets were nearly deserted in spite of the excitement caused by the Buck Creek gang.

Sam and Nevada paused a moment as they approached the saloon, and talked in low tones. Then they separated, Sam going to the front of the building and Nevada to an alley at the rear. Sam stopped again as he approached the door and carefully examined his gun.

In the saloon the pool and card games had come to a halt. At first the unusual hilarity was joined in with a roar, but it was soon sensed there was something more here than merely painting the town red. A few men stood close to the wall, and others were seated on a long bench near the pool tables. Two of them were holding cues, and Bert Wilson, who was freezing to four kings, tried in vain to induce the others to go on with a poker game.

Hank Miller, the proprietor, was behind the bar. He was looking very serious, but neither he nor his bartender made any attempt to restrain the gang from Buck Creek.

Directly between the two windows, facing the opposite wall, with the door on his right, stood Snake. Opposite him and a little to the left was Highpockets Lamont, a tall, slender individual with beady eyes and a long, hawk nose. To the left of the bar stood Spike Eagen, and at the other end was Drowsy Black, who seemed half asleep but could move fast enough when necessary.

Drowsy was the fastest gunman among them. He held a .44 in his right hand. The hammer was filed smooth, and he could thumb it with lightning speed. In the careful plan they had made, Drowsy was the one selected to fire the shot that would kill Burton.

It was a simple plan. They knew the shooting would bring the sheriff. As Burton approached, Snake and Drowsy were to begin quarreling. As the sheriff entered the room, they would begin to shoot, apparently at each other. The sheriff would be directly in the line of fire. They would swear that the quarrel was merely a joke, and the sheriff's death entirely accidental.

All of them had been drinking, but not enough to dull their faculties or to show their hands. Highpockets could see up the street through the window at the side of Snake.

"Look out for Burton, men!" he shouted. "I jest seen the lights go out in his office."

"Yeah," answered Drowsy, "mebbe he's goin' to put a stop to our little spree. *Ye-e-e-ow!*"

He raised his voice in a shrill, cowboy yell and emptied his gun into the ceiling. Then he stuffed fresh cartridges into the cylinder and waited with muscles tense.

A silence followed his outburst.

"You fellers had better calm down," began a cowpuncher, but he stopped as he caught a glance from Snake's eye. He swallowed hard, and then watched the door.

All eyes followed him. The four Buck Creek men had drawn their weapons and were waiting silently and expectantly.

Highpockets could see two men coming down the street from the sheriff's office.

"Burton's comin'!" he called. "Someone's with him, too. So you high-wranglin' waddies had better cut the rough stuff an' say your prayers."

"To hell with the sheriff," snapped Snake. "Who's afraid o' a little runt like him?"

"The sheriff's a runt an' a sneak!" said Drowsy. "He's a friend o' mine, an' anyone that says he ain't all right'll get his gizzard blowed out."

Both Snake and Drowsy were pretending to be very drunk. Snake fired twice into the ceiling.

"The sheriff's a runt an' a sneak!" he bawled. "I can lick any man that says different."

This was Drowsy's cue for a sharp rejoinder that was to start the fake battle, but he hesitated and waited for Burton to enter the room.

A strange silence followed Snake's challenge. All turned toward the door. It remained closed. Things were not going according to program. Had the sheriff got cold feet and stayed away? There was ample time for him to have reached the saloon since Highpockets announced that he had left the office.

The door opened a couple of inches.

Drowsy felt that he should go on with the quarrel. He licked his lips and glanced at his gun.

The crack in the door widened.

"You're a liar!" croaked Drowsy.

"You can't get away with that!" Snake cried. "No lousy cowpoke can call me a liar an' get away with it. Draw your gun!"

Drowsy's gun was already drawn.

They were to begin shooting at this stage of the game, but the sheriff did not enter, and the door remained slightly open.

Those in the room watched it as though fascinated. Snake and Drowsy apparently had forgotten their quarrel. There was a death-like stillness in the room, the only sound being the steady ticking of the big clock behind the bar.

Then the door swung open with a bang and in strutted old Sam Proctor.

He was bareheaded, and his hair hung low over his forehead. His keen eyes gleamed like two stars on a cloudy night. A huge chew of tobacco was in one cheek, and he carried his deputy badge high on his chest where it flashed belligerently in the lamplight.

"Howdy, boys!" he greeted cheerfully. "Don't let me interfere with the fight. Go right ahead an' shoot each other up. A good riddance all around, I'd call it. Hi, there, Snake! Sorry to see you got out o' jail. I'd think you'd be mighty glad to go to the pen an' stay there. It's a danged sight better'n livin' in Buck Creek."

He looked around the room. The four gunnies were standing with drawn weapons.

"Highpockets," said Sam, "you're a infernal idjit. Drowsy, you ain't got sense enough to punch dogies, to say nothin' of bein' a bad man. Spike, go on home an' tell your mother to put you to bed."

Then Sam strutted up to Snake who had lowered his gun.

"Jest to make a bad example," he orated, "an' to show the whole danged world that Elk City is a peaceful an' law-abidin' community, superior in every way to Buck Creek, I, Sam Proctor, depitty sheriff, hereby arrest Snake Simmons for creatin' a disturbance an' plottin' ag'in' the life o' the sheriff. I know all about it, Snake. Put up that gun!" He pulled his cedar-handled .45 with a lightning move.

Snake's answer was to shoot from the hip.

Sam staggered back as the gun crashed. He flung himself sidewards to the floor and rolled rapidly as Snake fired again. Then his .45 roared twice from his prone position.

The rustler's gun fell from his hand. He slumped forward, clutching at his chest.

A bullet from the other side of the room grazed Sam's ear, and he rolled behind the stove. He fired twice, and then lay still while he peered between the short legs of the stove, and tried to make out where the other men were hiding.

Highpockets was crouching behind the huge legs of a pool table, and Spike was behind the bar. Drowsy had not moved. He stood at one end of the bar and took careful aim at the side of the stove where Sam was entrenched.

There was the splintering crash of glass! Drowsy turned just in time to meet the barrel of Nevada's revolver that caught him squarely above the right ear. He sank to the floor and remained there.

Highpockets and Spike both fired as Nevada came through the broken window, but he moved so fast that both missed.

Nevada squatted at the end of the bar and peered cautiously around the corner. A shoulder came into view and disappeared quickly as his gun roared.

Sam was firing steadily at nothing in particular, and he was shouting his war cry. His motive was entirely strategic. He had upset a spittoon, and the contents had gurgled out on the floor. Sam wanted to go elsewhere, and was laying down a barrage before advancing to another position.

He loaded the gun, fired four times in rapid succession, and then crawled quickly to a card table, overturned it, and slipped behind. A bullet splintered the wood as he drew his legs out of sight. Two more came through the table top close to his head, and he lay flat on the floor.

"One o' them rannies shore knows how to throw a gun," he muttered to himself. Then he peered carefully around a side of the table. The top of a head was exposed at the corner of the bar and he fired. "Missed again, dog-gone it,' he complained. "I shore ain't as good as I used to be when it comes to slingin' a gun."

Again he peered around the table, trying to get a line on the positions of the other men. The non-combatants had gone through windows and the door. The room was left entirely to the four men.

Sam wondered who had done such good shooting when he crawled behind the table. Suddenly he had an inspiration.

"Nevada," he called, "are you the one over behind the bar?"

"Yeah, you bet your life!"

"Well, what in Gehenna are you shootin' at me for? Don't you know I'm a ally?"

"Gosha'mighty, I thought you was over behind the stove! Was you the ranny that jest missed the top o' my head?"

"Yeah. I can't shoot worth a cuss any more, Nevada. Dog-gone it, anyhow."

Nevada peered out from behind the bar at his friend. "Well, I wouldn't cry about it," he soothed. "You damned near blew the top o' my head off. What do you want to move around thataway for?"

"For a danged good reason. I upset one o' Miller's goboons, an' I can't swim."

A shot came through the top of the table. This time it was from the other side of the room. Sam used the hole to peek through with one eye.

Highpockets was peering around one of the big legs of the

pool table. His gun was held out ready for another shot.

Sam took aim through the bullet hole and fired. The wood was splintered, and the deflected shot ruined what Miller considered a work of art that was hanging against the wall.

Highpockets fired twice, and Sam lay flat on the floor. Then the old cattleman carefully raised a corner of the table and blocked it up with his plug of chewing tobacco.

The battle seemed to have formed into two separate duels, one between Highpockets Lamont and Sam, and the other between Spike Eagan and Nevada, who were concealed at either end of the bar. Sam could hear Nevada's gun roaring out shot after shot.

"The peaceful ol' bearcat." He grinned. "He ain't been in a ruckus like this since Heck was a pup. It'll loosen up his bones an' keep away the rheumatiz. I wonder if he remembers the time he beat One-Ear Baker to the draw over in the Flamin' Eagle Saloon at Las Animas."

Again Highpockets peered around the table leg. His hat and gun were exposed as he waited for a portion of Sam's anatomy to appear.

Sam was lying prone on the floor, but he had a good view under the upraised corner of the table. He peered over the sights of his gun at Highpockets's head, and then changed to the rustler's hand. He pulled the trigger.

Highpockets's gun flew from his fingers and he looked foolishly at a hand that was dripping red.

In a moment Sam was upon him, and the hot barrel of the big .45 was shoved into the back of his neck.

"This here ruckus is all over, Highpockets," he stated with great calmness.

The rustler began twisting a dirty neckerchief around his bleeding hand and said nothing.

"I got him, Nevada!" Sam called. "Hurry up with that

other ranny, 'cause I gotta be gettin' back to the ranch."

Nevada was growing tired of the duel he was fighting with Spike. The solid ends of the bar were riddled with bullets. Two windowpanes were smashed out, and a good business had been done in empty bottles that were piled beneath the bar. Otherwise there was no damage.

Spike lay closely to the floor and fired carefully.

Nevada knew if he didn't end matters, Sam would come to his aid, and he didn't want help. Old Sam had taken care of two of the gang, and Nevada felt it was up to him to gather in the others if he was to maintain a reputation as a deputy sheriff.

Drowsy moved slightly and began to moan.

"You better give up, Spike!" Nevada called. "There ain't no use in resistin' a officer o' the law, an' me an' Sam is both deputy sheriffs, an' we're out to keep everything quiet an' peaceful in Elk City."

There was no answer.

Nevada decided to end it one way or another. He flung his gun around the edge of the bar and fired three times at random. Then he pulled himself up to the bar and looked over the top. There was no sign of Spike.

"He's flat on his stomach," Nevada muttered.

He sprang to the top of the bar and tiptoed softly along it.

Spike looked up just in time to catch Nevada's boot square in the face. In another moment he was disarmed and helpless, with blood streaming from a cut in his forehead.

"Come on in, men!" called Sam. "Everything is peaceful in Elk City, an', if you don't believe it, jest try to start somethin'. Nevada, do you remember the big fight we had over in the badlands when we was all so shot up we had to be identified when we got home? We had some time in them ol' days. There ain't nothin' we can do that can bring 'em back."

It was a battered and sobered gang that mounted an hour later to return to Buck Creek. Nevada and Sam refused to lock them up. Snake Simmons was dead, his body lying beneath a blanket in the scarred and battered saloon. Highpockets's hand was in a cast. Spike and Drowsy had bandaged heads.

"Now, looky here," Nevada was orating. "You can go back to Buck Creek to stand trial for that rustlin' job, or you can beat it out o' the county, jest as you please. But the thing is shore, you can stay out o' Elk City, or we'll have you taken up for resistin' a couple o' danged good officers, shootin' up a good saloon, plottin' ag'in' the sheriff, an' everything else. Stay away from here an' don't ever come back again, 'cause, if you do, we might get mad an' treat you real rough."

They gave the sheriff's keys to a cowboy and asked him to turn loose the prisoner.

"No use talkin' to him tonight," Sam remarked. "It wouldn't do no good, an', besides, he'll prob'ly give us such a cussin' we'd have to put him back in jail again before we got him calmed down."

The two deputies went down an alley in order to avoid the crowd that had gathered. Neither of them had been injured, but Sam's old silver watch, that he prized above all earthly possessions, had been ruined by Snake's first shot.

They came out into a patch of moonlight near the general store.

Nevada suddenly drew his gun and emptied it at the moon. *"Ye-e-e-eow!"* he shrilled. "Sam, I sure feel like a kid tonight. Do you remember the time we painted up Harrisville an' run that whole damned posse into the White River?"

"I shore do, Nevada. An' the time Bull Radner tried to bluff you up at the Box S, an' you filled him so full o' lead he had to. . . ."

Sam paused as a buckboard drove up by the side of the store and stopped. There was a fervent embrace on the part of the two occupants. Then a girl sprang to the ground and ran up the steps to the living quarters above the store. The young man drove away in a cloud of dust.

"Nevada!" gasped Sam. "Did you see what that gal done?"

"I shore did, Sam."

"Kissed that young jackass right out there in the middle o' the street. Gosha'mighty, Nevada! What's comin' over these here young people anyhow?"

"I'm shore I don't know, Sam," groaned Nevada. "But one thing is certain. This here risin' generation is sure hard-boiled."

Next Door to Hell

The captain of the guard stopped Blin Bradley, cowpuncher and late placer miner, on the outskirts of Cuchara. *El capitán* was courteous.

"I am desolated, *señor*," he explained in broken English, "but His Excellency, the governor, has given strict commands that the *Señor* Bradley is not to enter Cuchara. It is feared that the peace and tranquility of our beloved city might be interrupted if the *Señor* were to do us the honor of paying us another visit."

The captain smiled and then continued in his persuasive voice.

"You understand, *señor*. A thousand pardons, but you comprehend that His Excellency's fears are not entirely ungrounded."

Blin grinned unhappily, pulled off his huge Mexican sombrero, and mopped a perspiring brow. It was a very hot day. His good-humored, rugged face, tanned almost to the swarthiness of that of the captain of the guard, was clean and newly shaved. He had anticipated a pleasant hour in the cool of a Cuchara *cantina,* before going onward in his search for the man who had betrayed and robbed him.

"Yeah," he agreed, "if I remember correct, I did have a little run-in with the old boy the last time I was here. I hope his whiskers growed out again all right. I only meant to singe 'em a little to chase out the cockroaches an' moths. I didn't know he had 'em all smeared up with inflammable grease."

His keen blue eyes rested contemplatively on the four guards who stood at attention in the middle of the road. As

96

though divining his thought, the officer smiled and shrugged his shoulders.

"I have sixty men in the town, *señor*. While none of them is to be compared as a marksman with the *Señor* Bradley, of whose wonderful skill we have been, alas, the unfortunate witnesses, yet you comprehend that sixty men firing a volley. . . ."

The cowboy's grin widened.

"Yeah, I get you, Captain. One of 'em might accidentally hit me."

"*Sí, señor,* it would be most regrettable."

"All right, *amigo,* you can tell Old Whiskerino he can take his *siesta* in peace. The *Señor* Bradley is headin' toward the border if he don't head for some other place."

The cowboy touched the sweat-streaked, tough-looking pinto with a spur, and turned to ride around the town.

"A thousand thanks for your courtesy!" the captain called. "Give my regards to your friend, *Señor* Archeluto."

Blin frowned. He intended to give *Señor* Archeluto something besides the captain's regards when he found him, for the *Señor* Archeluto had gone north with a sizable bag of gold dust and nuggets for which Blin Bradley had put in four months of back-breaking labor in an ancient streambed in the hills.

The cowboy was hurt deeper down than he cared to acknowledge when he learned that Juan Archeluto had not shown up at the town where he had gone to ship the gold. A *vaquero* reported that he had been seen near La Veta, that cesspool of humanity a few miles south of the border.

Blin had gone through hell for Juan Archeluto. He was attracted to the gentlemanly, soft-spoken Mexican *caballero* because Juan was everything that Blin was not. The cowboy had found in the carefully reared *caballero* all the education, refinement, and gentle courtesy that he himself lacked. Juan had admired the strength and the devil-may-care outlook upon life of the hard-riding, quick-shooting American. The two had been saddlemates nearly a year, and had called each other by one of the most sacred of all names: *friend*.

Blin's frown deepened as he rode over the rolling, rough hills that were eloquent with the desolation of a desert land.

"Friend, hell!" he muttered. "I ain't got no friends, an' I never will have again. Damn everybody!"

It was inconceivable that Juan had betrayed him.

An hour later he approached La Veta. No one would request him to ride around this little pest-hole, the headquarters of the American renegade, Mark Reeves. The dope-runners and female outcasts that inhabited the village welcomed anyone who had money. The *vaqueros* had a name for the place: Next door to hell! Blin had been here once before, and he knew he would have to watch his step in La Veta.

On the edge of the town was a doorless, windowless ruin of an adobe shack. Passing it, Blin turned suddenly as he heard a familiar voice.

"Help, help," it called in Spanish. "For the love of Christ, help!"

Spurring forward, the cowboy rode around the house. What he saw made him pull up short and set his lips in a grim line.

Juan Archeluto was lying there on the ground, a smear of blood across his forehead. His right arm was broken and dangling helplessly at his side. He was tied with a rawhide thong around his ankle, and the thong was fastened to a post at the corner of the house. Nearby was a red ant hill, and the vicious insects already were swarming toward him.

"Help, *señor*," he murmured. "For the love of . . . ah,

Madre de Dios, it is you, *amigo.* My friend, you have come in answer to my prayers to the Blessed Virgin."

The cowboy sprang from his pinto and slashed the thong. Gone were his anger and bitterness at the sight of the suffering of Juan, with whom he had eaten and slept and labored since the two had been thrown together a year before in the strangest of all midnight adventures.

The *caballero* sank back and closed his eyes.

"Juan," gritted the cowboy, "who did it?"

"It was . . . it was the *gringo,* Mark Reeves," he gasped. "They stole the gold, my friend, and I . . . I . . . but I cannot tell you now. I thank the Blessed Virgin that you have arrived, for I am not yet ready to die. I have work to do."

"Yeah," Blin answered gently, "I understand, Juan. I, too, thank your Blessed Virgin that I came in time."

Carefully he lifted the *caballero* and carried him into the ruin of a hut. Tiny lizards flashed out of the way. A scorpion lifted its tail sullenly and stalked into a crack in the wall.

Neither of the men saw a barefooted *peón* rise out of a clump of mesquite and slip away toward the village. Mark Reeves had left a spy to watch the dying agony of Juan.

Gently the cowboy laid the wounded man on the floor and cut away the blood-soaked sleeve. A red stream was oozing from a wound above the elbow that had smashed the bone. Blin bound it carefully with a sterile bandage that he carried for such emergencies. He did not attempt to improvise splints, but bound the arm close to the *caballero*'s side. The wound in the head was superficial and required but little attention.

Mark Reeves! Blin had heard many wild tales of this American renegade and his Mexican outlaws.

Cattle rustler, dope-runner, bandit, he had harried the border and the ranches with a ruthless hand. So far, the soldiers of the governor had been unable to bring him to the gallows he so richly deserved. It was rumored in certain places that his immunity was because of a fair division of the spoils with His Excellency, the governor, which was not at all improbable.

The cowboy knelt by Juan's side and poured water from a canteen through the parched lips.

"As soon as you feel able to ride, we'll go back to Cuchara. The doctor there will fix you all up. Just now all you got to do is keep cool an' don't fret. The big danger is fever, you know."

"I do not want to ride now, *amigo*," came the soft answer. "I want to lie here, for I am sick and faint. I have not your rugged indifference to pain, and am but a weakling. The gold is lost to us, Blin. Mark Reeves has it in his *cantina*."

The cowboy set his lips in a grim line.

"Mebbe that damned renegade will have another guess comin'," he gritted. "Keep cool, Juan, an' don't fret. As soon as the sun goes down, you'll feel better, and then we'll take the back trail for Cuchara and the doctor. In the meantime, I'll pay this Reeves *hombre* a little visit that mebbe he won't like."

The young Mexican looked adoringly at the cowboy.

"You come like an angel of mercy, *amigo*," he murmured. "You . . . you remember my little sister . . . and the bandit I told you about?"

"I sure do, Juan." There was a marked tenderness in the cowboy's voice as he spoke. "Yeah, I know all about it, and I know you've been lookin' for that man a long time."

"She was a lovely girl, Blin. I wish you could have known her. She was just out of the convent when the bandits captured our ranch and this man took her. I was bound and helpless. She . . . she died, *amigo*, after they had finished with her.

Even *Padre* Francisco, gentle man of God that he is, swore a great oath when we found her."

"Yeah, I understand, Juan," Blin soothed. "Don't think about it now. We'll find the skunk someday, and then you can settle with him in your own way."

"I found him today, my friend. He is this Mark Reeves. I went into the *cantina* after him, but he was too strong for me. I have not your strength, and your lightning speed with a gun."

In the *cantina,* word had been brought by the *peón* spy, Garcia, that a *gringo caballero* had set the victim free.

Mark Reeves, tall, broad, powerful, red-eyed, and unshaved, stood in his shirt sleeves before the bar. "The *americano* will come down the street," he told the five men and two women who were in the room. "We will bring him in here, for he is a dangerous enemy. He is the friend of Juan Archeluto, and I have heard much of him. You, Rosita, prepare to scream when he comes. He is the kind of fool that will run to a woman's aid when she screams. Lopez, stand by the door with your knife. Mind, you are not throwing at this *americano.* You are throwing at the image painted on the wall. He comes through the door and . . . *pouff!* It is too bad! You others stand by the bar. Be ready to shoot if Lopez should miss. We will kill this *americano* or he will cause trouble over the gold."

"He is riding this way," came the guttural voice of the *peón,* Garcia.

Through the dirty windows, they could see the tough-looking pinto trotting slowly forward. Blin Bradley was gracefully forking the saddle. The cowboy was coming straight toward the *cantina.*

"Now!" Reeves exclaimed. "Scream, Rosita!"

The girl was an olive-skinned, soft-eyed creature of not more than sixteen years. Shortly her charms would fade away, and she would be old, wrinkled, and a grandmother at thirty-five. But now a flash of youth and beauty was hers, and men desired her. For a moment she stood looking through the window.

"*Señor,*" she whispered, "he is handsome, this American. Please do not make me bring him to his death . . . like . . . like Stephano."

"*¡Caramba!*" cried the renegade. "You would fail me now? Scream, damn you, or I'll throttle you."

"*Señor,* I cannot!"

Like a tiger the huge bulk of Reeves leaped forward. He seized the girl by the throat and jerked her from side to side. His red eyes narrowed to mere slits in his face and his teeth were bared in a vicious snarl.

"Double-cross me, will you, you rat?" he raged.

"*¡Señor!*"

It was a cry from the *peón*, Garcia, who started forward with terror written in his eyes.

"*¡Señor! Por Dios,* pity! She is my daughter and she is with child. You know, *señor,* you promised to marry her. You promised before the *santo* of the Virgin."

The *peón* caught hold of the arm of the renegade. A blow of the huge fist caught him squarely in the face, and he went reeling into a corner. The shriek of the girl rang out on the still, dead air of afternoon, and it was not an assumed cry to draw the cowboy into the trap. It was the piercing, agonized scream of a woman in fear of her life.

Through the window they saw the pinto throw up its head. Blin Bradley vaulted out of the saddle, and came dashing toward the door of the *cantina.*

Lopez whipped back his hand, and the long knife glittered

for the death throw. Mark Reeves threw the girl to the floor, and stepped back against the wall. The three Mexicans crouched by the bar with guns drawn.

They were ready for Blin Bradley, the *americano* who would give trouble over the gold. They were not ready, however, for the smashing entrance of the 180 pounds of bone and muscle that catapulted through the door like an enraged bull. Gun in hand, so fast did the cowboy move that Lopez was caught off guard. The knife flashed through the air fully two feet behind Blin. It struck the wall and remained there, quivering.

A gun roared, and plaster was kicked from the wall within a few inches of the cowboy's head. He threw a bullet at the Mexican who had fired. The man went down, clutching his stomach. The others dropped their weapons and held their hands high. This *gringo* must be the devil in disguise!

Then Reeves came into the fray. With a bellow he hurtled forward, a .44 appearing in his huge fist.

Again Blin's gun roared. The weapon of the outlaw shot from his fingers and struck the floor. He paused and stared at a hand that began to drip red where it was grooved by the bullet.

"You *borrachón!*" he gritted. "You've done this to me?"

"I ought to have made it the heart, you damned reptile," Blin answered calmly, "but I couldn't do it. You belong to Juan Acheluto, and I ain't got the right to take you away from him."

With a few forceful words in Spanish, of which the *Padre* Francisco would not have approved, Blin lined the four men against the bar. The wide-eyed girl remained sitting on the floor where Reeves had thrown her. She was sobbing softly. The cowboy did not see Garcia, who remained motionless in the dark corner of the *cantina*.

"I came here for that gold, Reeves," the cowboy announced grimly. "In two minutes I'm going to begin shooting. First I'll notch your ears, an' then take off the end o' your nose, an' then. . . ."

"It will not be necessary," answered the outlaw. "I know when I'm licked. If any of these damned greasers was worth a cuss! But they ain't. Your gold is in there, mister, locked up in the desk."

He motioned toward an adjoining room, the door of which stood open.

Blin marched the four men ahead of him. The room was fitted up as an office, with a high, roll-top desk standing against the wall. There was no other furniture except a box filled with sawdust and three or four sag-bottomed cane chairs.

"Don't make a false move, any of you," the cowboy cautioned, " 'cause this here cannon is just itchin' to exterminate a few polecats. Bring out that gold, Reeves, an' lay it on the table. Be sure you don't grab a gun out o' the drawer. I'll be watchin'."

Blin stood, back to the door, menacing the four men with his gun.

Reeves turned to the desk and opened the middle drawer with a key. He moved slowly, for he had seen what the cowboy had not: the barefooted Garcia creeping through the door with a glittering machete in his hand.

"It's all here, mister."

Reeves drew a long, thin, canvas bag from the drawer. He lifted it as though it were very heavy.

A sixth sense seemed to warn the cowboy of the approaching danger. He turned just as the machete came down, the flat side of the blade catching him fairly on the head. Without a sound he crumpled to the floor.

★ ★ ★ ★ ★

The face of Mark Reeves leered above him as Blin struggled back to consciousness. The sunlight was filtering through a barred window and he found he was lying on a stone floor.

"This is an old *cuartel*, mister," came the mocking voice of Reeves. "It ain't been used for years, but I had a lock put on the door, and it'll serve the purpose once more. We will go away and leave you to your thoughts. I have put you and your friend together. It is better than feeding him to the ants, for you will die of thirst. I am leaving your gun with one load in the cylinder. It will be interesting to know which one of you will use it to kill the other so that he may drink his blood. I will come and look in at the window from time to time. It will be as good as a play."

With a laugh that was not pleasant to hear, the renegade went out and slammed the heavy plank door.

Blin sat up and looked about him. Seated with his back to the wall, a smile on his thin, sensitive face, was Juan. He laughed softly as the cowboy felt of a huge lump on his head.

"My friend, I am sorry," he said. "I should have let you take me to the doctor in Cuchara."

"Yeah, I sure balled things up, Juan. This here Mark Reeves is a nice little playmate."

"Yes, my friend, when a man of civilized race turns savage, he is. . . ." The *caballero* gestured with his free hand.

"Yeah, I know, Juan. He's a danged sight worse than the savages themselves. The question is . . . what are we goin' to do about it?"

"We can break out the bars of the window."

Juan's tone was so positive that the cowboy did not laugh.

"How do you mean, we can break 'em out?" Blin asked. "They look like oak bars to me, hard as boiler iron."

Juan answered: "You have the little glass you use to light the fires when we run short of matches."

In an inner pocket Blin had long carried a magnifying glass, small but powerful, to use when he was far from civilization.

"I'll be dog-goned," he murmured. "Mebbe you're right."

The sun was streaming into the old *cuartel,* making a great patch of barred light on the stone floor. The window was high and hardly two feet square.

Blin could see out it by standing on tiptoes.

"Yeah," he said as though speaking to himself, "I guess the boy is correct. We'll be out o' here in jig time. How are you feelin', Juan?"

"I am very well, *amigo.* The sickness I felt after being wounded is gone. When they brought you here, I thought you were dead, you lay so silent on the floor. I wanted to live only to avenge you . . . and my sister. Together we will live to hang this Reeves by the neck until he is dead."

Blin drew out the small glass. He held it with the bright spot of refracted light falling on the bottom of one of the bars. It seemed scarcely a moment before a tiny wisp of smoke curled up. Presently the dry wood broke into a flame.

The cowboy nursed it tenderly. Occasionally he blew it out and scraped away the charred wood, and then started it again. A deep notch was burned nearly through the bar. He repeated the process at the top, and with the other two bars that stood across the window.

"I can yank 'em out any time now, Juan," he said at last. "Whenever you're ready, we'll go out of here. And about that gold, so far as I'm concerned I don't give a damn about it. It's the adventure that appeals to me. I like goin' after gold when it's hid away in the hills. When I get it, the adventure is all over an' I lose interest."

"I know, my friend," the *caballero* answered softly, "and I, too, cared for it only that it might help me find the murderer of my sister. I felt that it would help me, and it did. It led me to him, and now its purpose has been served."

"All right, old top. If we sneak out of here in the daylight, they'll see us sure. We'll wait till dark and then find our horses an' hit the trail for Cuchara. Mebbe they'll let me go in if I prove to 'em that all I want is a doctor."

Slowly the blazing Mexican sun dipped down behind the jagged hills that were splashed with the harsh green of prickly pear and saguaro cacti. The deep, confusing twilight settled over the earth as Blin broke the bars and squirmed out through the window. It was not an easy task. The difficulty was increased by the sharp stumps of the oak bars. The cowboy realized suddenly that Juan, with one broken and helpless arm, could not get through that window.

"Wait a minute, Juan," he cautioned. "I want to look around."

He slipped around the *cuartel* to the door. It was locked with a huge iron padlock that nothing could touch short of a file, or a jimmy. He had heard of shooting a lock, but he thought a bullet could do no more harm than dent this one. Anyway, he didn't want to shoot. He had only one shell in the gun that Reeves had left him as part of the renegade's torture scheme.

"Juan," he called softly, "I've gotta get that key. I'll be back before long."

Then he made his way toward the *cantina* through the gathering gloom.

Mark Reeves was sitting at his desk, figuring with the stub of a pencil. The window was open, but the shade was drawn so that prying eyes could not see what Reeves was doing.

Before him was the long, thin bag of heavy canvas. The swarthy Lopez, with his knife in his boot, was sitting on one of the sag-bottomed chairs, smoking a long, thin cigarette.

"There's three hundred and seventy-two ounces of gold in this bag, Lopez," the outlaw chief was saying. "The way I figger, it's worth almost six thousand bucks, a nice little haul for you and me. The others will get only day wages, of course."

There was a timid knock at the door. Reeves frowned and shoved the bag into a pile of papers.

"Come in," he growled.

The *peón*, Garcia, entered silently followed by the soft-eyed Rosita. Reeves glared at them. He did not want to be disturbed, especially by these two.

"Well, what do you want?" he asked harshly.

"*Señor.*" The man cringed before the venomous glare of the master. "I . . . I served you well today, did I not, when I . . . when I vanquished the *gringo* who would have robbed you?"

"It would have been better if you had used the edge of the machete, Garcia. Otherwise it was well. What about it?"

Reeves was working himself into a passion, for he suspected what was coming.

"*Señor*, it is my daughter."

Reeves sprang to his feet with a curse, and the *peón* cringed like a whipped cur.

"She is only a baby, *señor*," he cried, "and you promised to marry her. Will you do so tonight?"

Reeves looked at the quailing figure of the man before him, and burst into a laugh. "Marry your slut of a daughter?" he cried in English. "No, not tonight or any other night." Then he spoke to the *peón* in his native tongue. "I was drunk, Garcia, if I made you such a promise. Take your daughter and go away from La Veta. Don't ever come back or it will mean death on the ant hill. I am through with both of you. I need you no longer."

"¡Señor!" The peón drew himself erect and there was a new light in his eyes, and a new ring to his voice. "You do this to me and Rosita?"

"Get out!" Reeves snarled. "Get out and don't come back."

"¡Caramba!" The voice was low with the hissing quality of the snake. "Señor, I am a Garcia, and will get revenge."

"Oh, you will!" Reeves's tone was as cold as tempered steel. "You want revenge, do you? All right, take it!"

His fist smashed fully into Garcia's face. The scream of the girl rang out as her father fell. Ignoring her, the renegade stepped forward and kicked the prostrate form into the corner.

"Here's your revenge, you damned Indian," he gritted.

The girl's cry of agony again pierced the stillness of the tropical night. Lopez grinned and puffed his cigarette.

The curtain over the window suddenly fell with a ripping sound, and Blin Bradley sprang into the room. Gun in hand he stood, his blue eyes boring into the face of Mark Reeves.

"You damned snake!" he snapped. "Say your prayers!"

Lopez sprang to his feet and his hand flashed downward to his boot.

"¡Señor!" The cry came from the girl.

Blin turned with the speed of the striking serpent.

Spang!

The bullet took Lopez fairly between the eyes. The knife flew wide and was buried in the wall. The outlaw pitched forward to the floor.

The cowboy's gun swept back and centered just above the renegade's belt buckle. There was no terror in Reeve's eyes.

"You forget, mister," he purred, "that there is only one bullet in that gun."

The pearl-handled .44 appeared in his hand. Blin sprang forward as the renegade's weapon barked out its message of death. His own gun came down on the outstretched hand and the bullet splintered into the floor.

The cowboy moved with the speed of the tiger, but, as Reeves's gun flew from his hand, his left fist shot up straight into Blin's jaw. A million stars seemed to flash about the room, and the cowboy gasped for breath as the huge arms caught him up in a crushing hug.

Blin was a master of the art of a rough-and-tumble fight, but in this test of sheer strength he was no match for the powerful outlaw. Slowly he was bent backward. Desperately he struggled to keep his feet. He struck out with short jabs. Again and again his fist smashed into the face before him, but he was off balance and his blows lacked the power to hurt.

The door swung back, and dark faces were framed in the opening.

"Get out!" Reeves snarled. "This is my killing."

His voice held the confidence of the victor. The faces disappeared, and the door closed.

The girl was cringing in a corner of the room. Garcia, lying prone on the floor, looked out with glittering eyes at this struggle that could have but one end.

The big hand of the outlaw came up and grasped Blin's throat. The cowboy, with a desperate heave, threw himself sideways, and for a moment the hold was broken. But again that terrible fist shot out. Blin sagged forward, his fists flying, and again Reeves rushed into a clinch.

With fists, feet, and head the cowboy struck, kicked, and butted, but the great barrel of a body before him seemed as hard as iron. Blin knew he was fighting a losing battle.

Again the relentless hand closed on his throat. The cowboy was shoved backwards. Strange, colored lights were whirling about the room, and a singing came into his ears.

He caught sight of the long, canvas bag lying among the papers on the table, and he thought of Juan, sitting helpless in the old *cuartel*. It was the gold that had caused Juan to be distracted. It had brought the cowboy to this pesthole in the hills, to La Veta—next door to hell!

With a mighty wrench he again broke the hold and stepped back. Reeves roared aloud as he sprang upon him. The cowboy's fists shot into the contorted face. Then the renegade had him by the throat, again pressing him backwards.

Blin's struggles grew feeble. He gasped for breath. He jabbed the face before him, but he knew there was no strength in his punches. The light was fading away. It was growing dark. A voice seemed to be calling something to him, but he could not understand. Perhaps Juan. . . .

He fell in a limp heap on the floor, and lay looking up at the vague features of the outlaw chief. A red fog seemed to sweep down around him, and he felt that he was floating upward into the sky.

A harsh laugh brought him back to the earth. Slowly his vision cleared.

Reeves was standing above him. The outlaw had picked up his pearl-handled .44 and was pointing it straight at Blin's face. He was leering at the cowboy with his battered eye.

"So this is the great Blin Bradley that twice took Juan Archeluto out of the place I prepared for him," the outlaw gloated. "You would make an enemy of Mark Reeves, would you? I might prepare a nice little exercise for you, where my *hombrecitos* would pull out your toenails and turn you barefooted in the desert, but I choose to kill you myself . . . now. See! Shall I count ten, and then shoot. Between the eyes you shall have it, as you killed Lopez."

The red fog again crept slowly down around the distorted face of the outlaw. His voice seemed to be coming from a great distance. Blin wanted to rise, but he was tired and faint and did not care. He heard the count come slowly from far away.

"Four, five, six . . . ," he heard, and then the voice surged out stronger.

Behind Reeves another form loomed, and the bloody visage of the *peón*, Garcia, appeared out of the red fog. Closer it came. Blin wondered if he were dreaming.

"Seven, eight. . . ."

The teeth of the renegade were drawn back in a snarl. He spat out the count with all the viciousness of a man who loves to torture and to kill.

"Nine. . . ."

There was a dull sound, like that of a meat cleaver on the chopping block.

The awful vision of a face divided in half appeared in the red fog, and Blin knew that Reeves would torture and kill no more.

"Thou are avenged, my Rosita," a voice spoke brokenly.

The fog slowly cleared, and Blin sat up. Garcia was helping the sobbing girl through the window, and the two disappeared in the darkness.

The cowboy struggled to his feet and looked about him. He shuddered at the object on the floor. Next door to hell! But he must have the keys!

His eyes caught sight of the canvas bag on the desk. Mechanically he picked it up, then found the keys, and a moment later stepped out into the night.

As though in a dream he found the two saddled horses, and led them up before the *cuartel*. The key grated in the lock, and he helped Juan out of the prison and onto the horse. Briefly he explained what had taken place.

Silently they rode away toward Cuchara, where a doctor would set Juan's broken arm and put soothing lotions on the battered face of the cowboy.

"The gold, Juan," Blin said softly. "I recovered it. Take it, my friend. You wanted it badly or you never would have brought it here."

"I brought it here?" There was surprise in the voice of the *caballero*. "Did you not know, my friend? Reeves and his men caught me on the road to town where I was going to ship it to the mint. I followed them here to retake it from them. I could not come back to you and tell you that, in my weakness, I had failed. I do not want the gold, *amigo*. Mark Reeves is dead, and I will return to my home. You will go with me, and we will do what you call punch the cows together."

Under his breath the cowboy cursed himself for doubting the friend at his side. Ahead were two vague forms walking along the road. They were Garcia and the soft-eyed Rosita. Blin pulled up as they came to the *peón* and his daughter.

"Here, friend," he said as he pressed a long, thin bag into the man's hands. "It is for Rosita. And you, also, can buy yourself another machete for the one you left back there in the *cantina. Adiós,* old *borrachón,* and good luck!"

The two friends rode onward into the night.

Feud Fight

Hugh Sadler knew just about what had happened when he saw Slim Hilliard riding in. Slim came jogging along the brink of a crumbling wash, and swung down beside the Flying D's chuck wagon.

"It's started," Slim said. "He's got a big camp of Hat Indians digging post holes across the head of the Little Moccasin. They got pretty near across today. Doesn't take long to finish up the job, knocking in posts a hundred at a clip."

The whole camp waited for Hugh Sadler to blow up, but he didn't. He didn't say anything at all. In a way, the silence with which he took it was more portentous than anything he could have said, for it meant that he had already decided what he should do if this news came in.

This was the right year for a fence play, and the right season, and even the right kind of day to hear about it. Hugh had held 2,000 head in the upper plains of the Sisaquoin as long as he dared, and now had them on the move through the weirdly unseasonable warmth of a Chinook.

The warm winds sent the prairie snows rushing off in gulches usually dry, and turned the flats into vast beds of mud. The weak cattle wanted to lie down in the mud, and once down they could hardly be got up. When finally prodded onto the trail, they were in an angry mood and fought all day long.

As if there wasn't mud enough, it had now begun to rain. Cowboys and livestock wrangled at each other in a good old-fashioned drizzle-drizzle—all day, all night, all the next day—and the only end to it they could look forward to was a bitter-winded freeze. There was rain in the coffee, rain in the beans, rain running down from saturated shirt tails inside everybody's *chaparejos*. Not a soul had brought a slicker.

Just now most of the cowboys were hunched on their heels about the smudging and sputtering fire, but some few were frankly sprawled on their backs in the muck, certain that they could get no wetter and no filthier than they were. A couple of these now sat up, but nobody said anything. All of them knew what this move meant. Most of them had ridden for the Flying D for a long time.

They were in for a siege of violence and change. The range could go along for just about so long, its cow outfits thriving in peace through good years. But the outfits kept growing, their herds swelling with prosperity, just as the big steers filled out and bulged with the strength of the good grass that came on forever. When the outfits had grown enough so that they crowded one another, something had to bust. They had come to one of the bust-ups now.

Hugh Sadler walked a little way out toward the remuda and Indian-signaled the horse wrangler to bring him a pony. After a minute Alf Reedy, Hugh's foreman, turned his back on the others and walked out to where Hugh stood.

"Hugh," Alf Reedy said, "Hugh, you're a young man yet. Well . . . twenty-eight is young, to an old buck like me. But you built this outfit up good. Don't you throw it away."

"I told him," Hugh said, "I wouldn't allow that fence."

Both men knew the reason for Homer Willard's new fence line. That it would touch Flying D land hardly mattered. The cow country was getting crowded; if Willard's Running W was to expand much more, someone had to be crowded out, and the Clintons were the natural pick. Every year the Clintons drove their Circle Dot cattle down the valley of the Little Moccasin to the Bull Elk Breaks; by this drive they saved hundreds of head at the tag end of a bad winter, or gave the cattle a good start in an easy year. Both Hugh Sadler and his foreman knew that Willard had timed his play to cripple the Circle Dot when the Clintons could stand it least.

"Don't throw it away, Hugh," Alf repeated. "You got a stubborn streak. But stubborn don't win. I've seen you bluff him time after time. But you've bluffed enough. You cain't bluff him now."

"The freeze will hit us any hour," Hugh answered him. "It's too late for the Clintons to swing their drive. If Homer Willard can hold the Little Moccasin fence line, it busts the Circle Dot."

"Sure he can hold it. You cut Willard's wire, you got to fight. They'll git their hayride stomped to hell and gone, they make a move through that fence. The point is . . . it's the Clintons this bears down on . . . not on us. And this is one year we cain't afford to fight no other outfit's fight."

Typical of this lonely range, neither man spoke of legal rights. Futile to look in law books to find out whether or not Willard had a right to close a trail that had always been open, futile to appeal to a chair-bound political appointee ninety miles away, when disaster could so swiftly outrun the slow wheels of what little law they had.

"I know what you're going to say," Alf griped. "You need the Circle Dot for a buffer brand. If the Clintons are squoze out, we're squozed next. And when it comes to now, we ain't in no shape for triflin'. Start trouble with the Running W, and the finish is plain to see."

Hugh said: "Alf, I won't have that fence."

Alf Reedy opened and shut his mouth a few times in a baffled way. He could have understood it in Hugh's father. Bob Sadler had been hot-headed and slashing reckless, liable to push open battle against any brash odds, and win it, too.

Hugh had his father's dark brows, long chin, and high-boned face, but Hugh was reasonable to the point of easy-going. Raising hell at all costs—like jumping onto Homer Willard's Running W over a fence that was no hurt to the Flying D— that wasn't natural to him. Alf sensed some hidden, strange motive here. It troubled him the more because this was not the first time he had seen something of this kind crop up in Hugh, unexplained.

"Look," he said, taking a reaching liberty, "have you, by any chance, been seeing that Clinton girl?"

Hugh Sadler said mildly: "Well, let's see. The feud fight was nine years ago. She was about eleven, then. I suppose I've seen her since, maybe six, seven times. But not to speak to, Alf."

"It beats me," Alf mumbled. The horse-wrangling kid brought up Hugh's pony, and they walked back to the fire. Alf threw on Hugh's saddle one-handed, by the horn, while Hugh put on the split-ear bridle. Alf said: "If so, chances are you aim to go jaw Homer Willard, some more of us better go along."

"Don't aim to jaw him. Just aim to tell him." He stepped into the saddle, and his rein hand was busy quieting the fret of the cold-backed pony as he gave final orders: "Break out your drive three, four hours before daylight. Don't push 'em fast but push 'em steady, and push 'em long. We'll need most hands elsewhere, right short after tomorrow."

Alf Reedy looked as nearly savage as he ever let himself. Cattle were everything, first and last, to Alf. "If the freeze catches 'em laying down, like tomorrow night, before they're into the shelter of the breaks, we cain't spare no hands for no fence fight. A big share of them dogies is fixing to have to be tailed up by hand. Or else they'll never get up."

"That'll be too bad," Hugh said.

"Just one other thing . . . I seen the Clintons' old man Weatherby. The Clintons taken it in their heads *we're* building that fence." This was Slim Hilliard, belatedly rounding out his report. "Either that, they figure, or else we've thrown in with Homer Willard. They're fit to be tied."

Hugh shrugged. "Well, that's natural."

"You look out for Ted Clinton, Hugh," Alf urged him. "You watch him close, case you meet him on the trail!"

"Ted's all right," Hugh said. "You can't scarcely blame him." He rode away.

Looking after him, Alf Reedy tipped his hat forward to scratch his head. "How comes a man to be so partial to his blood enemies thataway?"

An old man, who was trying to keep a lit pipe in his mouth by smoking it upside down said: "The winners generally forget fust. It's the losers remembers good."

Alf shook his head. "More to it'n that. Got to be. There was something funny about that feud fight, mark me, something funny we don't know, and nobody knows, only Hugh."

They were thinking about the fool things Hugh Sadler had done from year to year—things that sometimes cost him plenty, and had no reason, except that it seemed he was dead set on saving the Clintons from being crowded out. Everybody knew about something like that Hugh had done—except the Clintons who wouldn't believe it if they heard.

The cowboys couldn't understand it. Those of them who knew that Hugh never went near the Clinton girl supposed that there must have been some treachery by the Sadlers in the feud fight, so that Hugh was conscience-ridden. Like as if maybe the Sadlers had shot down the Clintons while they had their hands up.

"I wish," Alf Reedy said, "he wouldn't go riding into the Running W layout and raise hell, all alone like that."

As it was to turn out, he was going to get his wish. Hugh Sadler did not reach Homer Willard, or the home ranch of the Running W to which he had set out.

He rode southeast toward the Little Moccasin, over familiar trails. It was coming dusk when Hugh met a two-bronco buckboard on the old Silverpost stage road, and rode no farther.

By the swing of the driver's shoulder to the lurch of his rig, as much as by the horses he drove, Hugh recognized him a long way off. He pulled one buck-gloved hand from his pocket, so that both would be visible. He carried a long, loose rein, so that his hands were now together, high on his wishbone, as he rode. And he kept on, expecting to pass as he and Ted Clinton always passed each other—Ted watching him sidelong and whistling tunelessly to himself, Hugh with eyes straight ahead, without change in expression or his pony's pace.

But Ted Clinton pulled up, hunching the ends of his driving lines under him to free his hands. "All right, Sadler!"

"What do you want, Ted?"

"I've been to the Little Moccasin. I've seen your fence. Take care of yourself!" He swung his shoulders to reach behind the seat, and a carbine whipped up.

Hugh Sadler was saying—"Wait, Ted! Wait . . . !"—as the carbine spoke.

Hugh's shoulders cupped forward with a convulsive jerk. He swayed sideways from the saddle stiffly, and pitched into the rutted mud.

For a space of time that he could not have judged but which was actually about an hour, Hugh was mainly aware that he was struggling hard for his breath. When he was conscious, which was not all of the time, he knew that he was bleeding, and that the jolt of the buckboard was tearing at his chances.

By the time they reached the Circle Dot, however, and he lay on a bed in the Clinton house, Sadler knew that Ted Clinton had not finished him this time.

Ted Clinton was standing over him, and beyond Ted was his sister—the two who were all that were left of the Clintons. Hugh had known both of them when they were knee-high to a tall Indian, little as he had seen of them since. When he looked at Ted, Hugh could see Gaylord Clinton. Ted seemed to be about seventeen now; Gay had been only a couple of years older than that when he was killed in the feud fight, nine years ago.

Ted was not as tall as Gay had been; he was more rugged in the shoulders, and more snubbed in the nose. And he didn't look as if he laughed as much as Gay; Gay had more fun out of life than anybody Hugh had ever seen. But Ted recalled Gay in the way he moved, and in the throaty shaping of his words—in a hundred ways you couldn't put your finger on, but which sometimes made Gay himself seem to be back there for a minute.

Carolyn Clinton, Ted's sister, said soberly: "Ted, you've all but killed him."

"Reckon my thumb must have slipped on the hammer. God knows I sure aimed to kill him."

"You'll have to ride for Doc Haversham," Carolyn told her brother. "He can at least probe the bullet out."

"He isn't carrying the bullet, Sis. It tumbled sideways. Here . . . you can see where it took out near the whole side of his coat. Doc can't do nothing."

Hugh Sadler spoke, but faintly, for he could hardly get his breath: "Bum shooting Ted. You hurried it."

Ted said, through his teeth: "Well, anyway, I took a couple of his ribs."

Carolyn drew her brother away then, and they went out of the room, but Hugh could hear their voices—Carolyn's very low, Ted's angry and impatient.

"We can't take him home, Ted. We don't dare move him, the way he is."

"What if the Flying D cowboys read the trail, and find him here?"

"Read a trail," the girl said, "in all this rain?"

Carolyn Clinton came back to Hugh alone. She stripped off his shirt, bathed and bandaged him, and afterward got him between clean sheets.

So this was the girl, he was thinking, with whom everyone—Homer Willard, Alf Reedy, all of his own outfit, probably—linked his name. He was glad to have a look at her.

He could see why people thought of her as a possible reason for what was considered his folly. There was enough family resemblance between Carolyn and Ted—and Gay Clinton—so that you could see she was their sister, all right, but her grave-faced quiet separated her from them so that she didn't suggest them at all. There was a quiet in her eyes as if she had seen a long way ahead for a long time, and had become so used to looking at what she saw there that she could look at it without bitterness. Yet it was not an acceptance that was the same as defeat.

For the next hour she was in and out of the room a good deal, and during this time Hugh heard Ted ride away. When his side would let him, he watched Carolyn as she came and went, and wondered about her.

He wondered if she were pretty. Often you couldn't tell, with even the prettiest of them, until they smiled. Carolyn didn't look as if she smiled very much.

She *could* laugh, though. He remembered seeing her two years ago—about the last time he had seen her. She had been sitting in a row of cowboys on a fence, watching the bronco-pitching contests over at the settlement, and she was having a good time. She'd been laughing then, all right; it lighted her up and changed her no end. Hugh thought he hadn't ever seen anybody look livelier or happier.

Toward midnight Ted had not returned. Carolyn came and sat in a rocking chair by the window in the room where Hugh lay. She was watching the sleeting, windy night.

Hugh said: "No call to sit up with me. Better go on to bed."

She allowed herself a brief quirk of a smile. It was the only time she smiled. "You're in my bed."

He managed to grin, not at her, exactly, but in a general way. But the brief flicker of light was gone; nothing in her face answered him.

A little later, listening to the big breathing of the wind in the cottonwoods, he said: "I remember those trees when they were no bigger than my finger, how you used to carry water to them every day."

Carolyn said, in her low, even tones: "You have a good memory." It was as if she had said: *I remember it all. There isn't anything I've forgotten, or expect to forget.* And he knew the feud fight was in her mind. He supposed that nothing else could be expected in her mind, when he was within her attention.

So he said now: "I remember a whole lot. I remember too much. Just about the plainest of anything, I remember your face that day. The look on it, I mean. Sometimes I've thought I'd just as lief trade places with Gay, to take that look away."

She said strangely: "I remember your face, too."

He wished he knew what that memory was. He couldn't

122

see how his face in that moment of the guns could have shown anything but shock, and compassion, and grief. But he knew it wouldn't get him anything to ask. He closed his eyes, too weak to go on.

He woke toward morning with his brain cool and clear, and the worst of the trouble in his side was quiet.

He saw at once that Carolyn was still sitting by the window, asleep now, in the rocking chair.

He told himself: *I couldn't have done any different. Even if I knew it would bust the Flying D. I'd have to do the same, if it was to do again.*

As he lay there now, he was living over the feud fight again, remembering it all, step by step, more clearly than he had remembered it for years. The cause was plain, even to himself; it was Carolyn who made the memories come back. He did not know this girl at all, yet her physical nearness had this peculiar effect. Once, while bandaging him, she had leaned so close to him that her hair had brushed his face, and instantly he was living the feud fight again, as if it had been today. For the girl had played a part in that fight, where Hugh was concerned, which neither she nor anyone else ever suspected.

Now he was lying in the Clinton house, in Carolyn Clinton's own room. These were the things she lived with and touched every day, this was the air she breathed. Even the bed on which he lay—his blood must be in its mattress—was her bed. And it was as if his unfired gun were in his hand again, and the smoke from his father's gun and Gay Clinton's was sharp in the sun-baked smell of the air.

The Clintons and the Sadlers should never have fought at all. The two families—both traced back to Kentucky—were of the same breed, the same ways of thinking, the same class, well suited to understand each other. They should have stood together against the range, and for a long time they had.

The difference started between Gay Clinton and Dick Sadler. Dick, a cousin of Hugh's father, was some older than Gay, but just as explosive and free of tongue.

When their quarrel had drawn the families in, Hugh's father had decided it had gone on long enough. He talked Dick out of it, and all three Sadlers had ridden over to the Clintons of a Sunday, with no other intention in the world than to apologize, if necessary, and make peace.

They rode into the Clinton layout without any formality, and tied their ponies at the rack that stood out in front of the house, just as they always had done. But the Clinton men, of course, didn't know what they had come for. Through the screen door Hugh Sadler saw Doug Clinton whip his gun belt around him before he stepped out.

Carolyn Clinton was sitting on the floor of the gallery, a lot of hollyhock heads around her. She was ten or eleven then, and her brother Ted was eight, as Hugh had judged it, or maybe both a little younger. Anyway, Carolyn was still playing with dolls. She was making little ladies out of the hollyhock blossoms by tying waistlines with thread, and Ted had been watching her. A whole circle of hollyhock ladies were dancing on the gallery floor.

As Ben Clinton came onto the gallery, his hands still at the gun belt he had just buckled, he tossed the children a curt order to go to the kitchen and stay there. But he was used to being obeyed, and in his preoccupation did not notice that this time he was not. As the Sadlers came up, the Clinton men were standing along the edge of the unrailed gallery, the children forgotten, and a fight that would not have been long remembered if it had happened among saddle tramps in a cow-town saloon was made into something else.

Gay, the irresponsible, spoke first, challenging the Sadlers with a demand to know what was wanted now. Dick snapped back that he didn't have to jump down their throats, and Gay made some mention of varmints. And so in the first minute their voices were up, and nothing could have saved what followed except for the Sadlers to have backed away—which, since they'd never backed up for anybody, they didn't know how to do.

Hugh could still hear his father's voice plainly, as plainly as if it were here in the room. He was saying . . . "Easy, Dick! Easy, Dick! Look, Gay. . . ."

He was still saying that when Gay's gun whipped out fast, faster than those watching for it could have expected. And he had already fired two wild, mad shots at Dick, from so close that it seemed nobody could have missed, when Dick brought him down with the only shot he fired.

Ben Clinton's gun ripped out, but a shot from Hugh's father stopped him in the same instant. He went to pieces from the waist down, and pitched off the gallery.

Doug Clinton had squatted sideways on his heels to spoil Bob Sadler's shot. What it spoiled was his own draw, and he collapsed there without firing. Then abruptly all guns were still.

Gay Clinton lay on his back, his legs trailing off the gallery. One of Gay's hands was flung out, palm up, and his fingers were slender, almost as graceful as a girl's. A little way from his hand the hollyhock ladies danced. Some of them had been knocked over by the lunkish steel mass of Gay's fallen gun.

After the feud fight the luck seemed to go out of the range, even for the victors. Hugh's father was killed within the year, under a hill stampede, and soon afterward Dick Sadler died under a somersaulting horse. Ben Clinton lived two years, although he never walked again. When he finally died, his wife did not long survive him. It was as if the feud fight had turned on all the disaster there was.

The Circle Dot went on, run by old man Weatherby—intensely honest, unquestioningly faithful, with an uncommonly keen judg-

ment of livestock, but even at the time of the fight he had been pretty old, long out of most of his teeth. Only Homer Willard expanded and prospered as expected. Young Hugh Sadler, boss of the Flying D, had a little better than held his own, but old man Weatherby had proved no match for the rapacious owner of the Running W. All of them had reason to remember the feud fight every day of their lives.

But sometimes it is meaningless little things that stick in the mind, and what stuck in Hugh's mind was the hollyhock ladies. Somehow those little pink, flouncing dollies dancing on the barren boards made everything ten times worse. He never again set eyes on a hollyhock without feeling queer.

And plainest of all, he remembered the terror in Carolyn's face—stark, white, pitiful terror in the face of a little girl. That was the "something funny" that Hugh's own outfit didn't know about the feud fight. It was what underlay Hugh's folly in giving the Clintons the breaks for a long time afterward, in a way those closest to him could not understand, and earning himself the name of a fool.

It was why the presence of Carolyn Clinton in the room brought the feud fight back with a keen clarity of detail. For, although no one else might have recognized her, to him she was still identifiably the little girl with the hollyhock ladies, whose whole life the Sadler guns had changed before her eyes, past imagination or recall.

That day Hugh was worse, sometimes dizzily fevered. All day long he heard horses, coming and going around the Clinton corrals, ridden hard. Something was happening, and happening fast. Ted came, glanced in at Hugh, and left again. Old man Weatherby stuck in his bald head once.

Nobody told Hugh anything. He tried to question Carolyn, but learned nothing. Presently he knew he wasn't going to learn anything. He lay as quietly as he could, saving his strength, but his mind fretted to a lather. About his only chance was that Alf Reedy would guess what had happened and look for him here. But the upshot of that would be that Alf Reedy would probably jump down with all hands, and clean out the Clintons in a fight that would be a horror. Hugh didn't know what to hope, except that some miracle would break.

Carolyn was in and out all day. Sometimes she sat on the edge of his bed, and spoon-fed him buttered mush and soup. By these intervals he was able to guess the time of day. He thought: *There couldn't be any lovelier thing than she'd be, if only she were happy. But this house is full of nothing but hate. Hate is what they live and breathe, around here.* Then a little later he thought: *No, the girl doesn't live hate. I wouldn't blame her if she did, the same as her mother. But she doesn't.*

The rain ended that night, and a bitter wind howled over the prairie. Two hours after dark Ted came storming in, his nose blue but his cheek bones ablaze with the bite of the frost, and Hugh picked up his first news of what was happening on the range.

Ted came clanking into the room where Hugh lay, because his sister was here. He disregarded Hugh completely; the wounded man was given a weird sense of not being there at all.

"They've fallen out!" Ted shouted. "The Running W has busted with the Flying D!" Even the set of his boots was triumphant as he stood untying his muffler. "There's been an open fight at the upper end of the Little Moccasin. One of the Running W 'punchers was hurt, and one of the Flying D . . . we don't know who or how bad. The Indians that were building the fence have gone home. There's a dead Flying D cow horse by the Moccasin fence, and the Flying D chuck wagon has been left stand over on Dog Flats, and the camp broke up."

Carolyn said: "Did you find out how it started?"

"My horse went home," Hugh said, "that's all."

"We don't know yet," Ted answered his sister. "We don't care a hoot, either! It's just a falling out among thieves. A bunch that's rigged up a dirty deal always goes to pieces when the ringleader drops."

"He's going to get well," Carolyn said.

"Too bad," Ted said. "Look, now . . . I don't know just what we better do. If this thing don't go haywire, it should wipe out the Flying D, and hurt Homer Willard at the same time. I'm aching to throw in and kick the hell out of some of 'em . . . either side. But all I can do is hold ready, and wait, and try to keep it from getting out Sadler is here."

"If the Flying D is done for," Hugh said, "the Circle Dot is finished, too."

Ted ignored half of that, but answered: "You can begin getting used to it. Your Flying D is gone."

"Yes," Hugh said without emotion. "It looks so. But I could save it, and you, too, if I could only get up from here."

Carolyn said: "That fence was hanging over us last year, and the year before. When it isn't that, it's something else. Year after year, hanging on the ragged edge of ruin. . . ."

Ted said fiercely: "It's always been their game to squeeze us out between them, that's why! The Flying D and the Running W has worked stirrup to stirrup, always, on just that one thing . . . to force us over the edge. But they've split up now, with their ringleader out. Maybe it's the turning point, Sis!"

Hugh said: "I didn't build that fence. It isn't true I threw in with the Running W, Ted, this year or any year. I've fought Willard as hard as you."

"I even caught you riding to Willard's home camp."

"I was going there. I aimed to tell Willard the fence couldn't stand, without he fought me, and it wouldn't have been the first."

"Oh?"

"That's why my cowboys have pitched into him now," Hugh said. "They know what I aimed to do. So they blamed Willard when my empty horse came home."

"Well," Ted said with contempt, "you don't mean to tell me."

"Willard and I never worked together a day. I've bluffed him when he was stronger than me and knew it, but couldn't bring himself to face the losses he'd take in a war to break me. But he'll break me if you keep me here. After that you'll see fence, you'll see squeeze! The Circle Dot won't outlast the Flying D a year."

"We'll take our chances," Ted answered dryly.

"I can put a check on him, even yet. I can hold off this war, and stop that fence, like I was setting out to stop it when you whacked me off my pony. But I can't do anything unless you let me tell you this . . . in all my life, I never made one move against the Circle Dot."

"He lies," Ted said, "as easily as he breathes."

And then Carolyn raised her face to her brother. Her words were so low that they could hardly hear her speak, but what she said was dynamite, to them both. She said: "I believe him, Ted."

Brother and sister looked at each other strangely for a long moment. Ted looked as if he'd been hit between the eyes. He shouted: "You gone out of your head?"

Old man Weatherby came hurrying in just then, with the stalking lurch of the aged horseman, and his sunken eyes were alight. "There's a glow in the sky to the northwest!" In his excitement his words whistled and fuzzed through his toothless gums. "Them Flying D rough-heads has hauled coal-oil drums and set fahr to them piles of fence posts!"

Hugh said: "Those boys are forcing on into a showdown. You'll see all hell busted loose by morning."

Ted Clinton's face was bright with savage elation. "I sure hope so!" He jerked down the brim of his hat and went stomping out, his spurs ringing, and Weatherby followed.

Carolyn called sharply: "Ted, where you going?"

He shouted back: "I've got to know what's going on! I'll sleep at the Cotton Notch camp, if I get time."

Experimentally, driven by an inner desperation, Hugh Sadler half raised himself, but soon fell back.

She said without expression: "You'd much, much better lie still."

"Willard will seize onto the burning of those posts. He'll claim the Flying D is marked outlaw by that, and pretend to swear in his riders for law deputies. The whole Running W will pile into the saddle. Don't you know all that?"

"Lie quiet, Hugh. There's nothing you can do if you could ride."

"I'll tell you exactly what I could do. I could raise up the Three Bar, and the Rafter Box, and the C Seventy-Seven. There's a dozen outfits that will stand with me if they can be reached. But Alf Reedy won't send until too late. I know him, and I know he won't send."

"Maybe he will."

"For God's sake," he begged her, "listen to me! Help me get up from here! Get me the buckboard. I can. . . ."

She said nothing, and didn't look at him. She was at the window, and he knew she was watching the distant glow of fire. But she shook her head with such finality that he gave up, and closed his eyes.

When he opened them, he caught her watching him, and

he experienced a shock of surprise, aware that what he had seen in her eyes for an instant was pity. It surprised him that his wound should have that effect. Then suddenly he knew that it was not his wound. This girl was seeing deeper than wounds or dollars, and saw something beyond his reach. He even wondered if she knew about something that was happening on the range that he didn't know.

Her eyes returned to the sky glow, but after a moment she left the window and came to his side.

"Hugh, were you telling the truth?"

"When did any Clinton believe any Sadler?"

"I don't know why I believe you. But I do."

He stared at her, and said nothing.

"I haven't ever understood," Carolyn said, "why Homer Willard twice started that fence, then gave it up. Why did you do it, Hugh?"

He tried no propitiation. "What difference does it make why? I didn't want it there, that's all."

"Why did you buy the Padlock water hole from Willard . . . then leave it open?"

"Some of my stock get over that way, sometimes."

She said slowly, as if to herself: "Every year it's been something, something that none of us could understand or explain. . . . All this long time. . . ."

She was staring at him strangely, so intently that she seemed to have lost all awareness of herself. She did not seem to know it when tears welled up, and ran down the smooth planes of her cheeks.

Suddenly she glanced about her, a little wildly, he thought, and quickly left him. He watched for her to return, but she did not. After a while he thought he heard her go out of the house.

Hugh listened for a long time, but the house remained

131

silent, empty, under the wind. After an hour he got himself into a sitting position, and got his feet to the floor. When he had stood up, he leaned against the wall for some minutes before he could trust himself to the open floor.

He found his clothes, and after a long effort got into them, although the boots nearly licked him. In a closet he found a rifle, and checked its load. He made it to the door.

There he stopped, and for an interval stood leaning upon the rifle, as still as if he listened. Then his shoulders hunched forward, his knees sagged, and he went to the floor slowly, his two hands sliding down the rifle barrel as they slipped their grip.

The Clintons' black cook heard the weapon rattle to the floor. He came and picked Sadler up in his arms and got him back into the bed.

It was morning, but still dark when Carolyn came in. She came directly to the room where Hugh lay, and turned up the light. She looked cold, and pale with fatigue, as she stood looking down at him, pulling off her gloves. Then she leaned closer over him to make sure that he was awake.

"Are you all right?"

He repeated huskily: "All right."

She sat down beside him, and her fingers rubbed her eyes. "I've sent a rider on a blood pony to look for Ted," she told him. Her voice was very tired. "I've raised up the Drakes, and the Rawlinses, and the Gundersons . . . some of them have gone for the Three Bar and the Larry K. The bigger half of a hundred cowboys ought to be at your place by now. I sent old man Weatherby with our few boys last night."

"You sent old . . . ? Carolyn, what's happened?"

"The Circle Dot is backing the Flying D." Wearily she slid from the chair to the floor, rested her arms on the edge of the bed, and laid her head on them. "I'm dead-beat, Hugh."

"Why?" He was unable to comprehend or believe. "Carolyn, why have you done this?"

"I don't know why. Any more than I know why I believe you. I guess I've never had much luck at hating you, or blaming you, or even distrusting you, Hugh."

He thought about that for a long time, but his amazement at the unforeseen, the unimaginable, did not decrease. "What about Ted?" he asked at last.

"We can't always please everybody, Hugh. He'll come to it in the end."

He was quiet for a long time. He couldn't think of anything that seemed adequate to say. But presently he touched her head, and then, perceiving that she seemed to be asleep, he let his fingers rest in her hair.

"This is a miracle," he whispered. "This is an Indian medicine, like nothing ever seen before."

She astonished him by answering him drowsily: "I think so, too."

When he had again overcome surprise, he said: "You're the magic in the miracle. You're all the magic there is." But this time she was really asleep.

A little after daylight Ted came up at the gallop. Carolyn's eyes opened, with the slam of the outer door. But she did not change her position, and the quiet of her face did not change, as her brother came in, then checked in mid-stride to stand bewildered.

Thanks to a Girl in Love

Old Man Coffee turned his hat in his hands and fidgeted. "Maybe I shouldn't horn in," he stated superfluously. "But. . . ." He trailed off in some confusion since the loneliness of hunting mountain lions for bounty had dried up Old Man Coffee's social graces.

Through the window of the little shack Mora Cameron's grave gray eyes stared at the mouth of a shaft perpetually murmuring with the dogged clamor of double-jack and drill. She said absently: "We're going to have to fight the water in Number Three."

There she went, thought Old Man Coffee, even now, while she was facing this thing that was almost too much for her, some part of her mind was mining still. Mora had taken over the Golden Eagle when her father had died in a cave-in of rock and in three years had seemed to prove that she was born to a curious success. To Old Man Coffee, though, the girl looked uncommonly soft-skinned and fragile in that gaunt mining-camp environment. He had watched her grow up—known her all her life—but he could never get used to this thing of a twenty-four-year-old girl's being a mining boss.

"It's Curt's black mood, I lay this to," Coffee said. "It's got so his best friends haven't dast go near him."

He had been half expecting Mora to boot him out, but he saw now that she wasn't going to. Perhaps she had the yearning of an inarticulate and mostly silent soul to talk about Curt and herself. She sat dreaming out the window, and the old lion hunter knew that she was picturing Curt Morse,

134

strapping big, with rocky shoulders fit to step off under a 500-pound pack. And Coffee was astounded to see that her face was tender. She was thinking of that big, hard-rock youngster as one thinks of a child!

"That sure must have been a good old snorter of a scrap you two had," Old Man Coffee offered gingerly.

"Yes," said Mora.

"I suppose you offered to show him how to run his mine?"

Mora shot him a gray glance. "Maybe I did." She pressed her hands to her face wearily, then let them fall again.

All this was the natural result, Old Man Coffee supposed, of the girl's running a better mine than the man. The fact that the Golden Eagle was paying out while the Morse Mine was not was only partly the fault of Curt Morse's inexperience with special local conditions. But, of course, Curt could not see that.

"Seems like . . ."—Old Man Coffee's hat, which he was still turning around and around, for a moment seemed struggling to escape his hands—"seems like you should ought to go and see him."

A moment passed, while, outside, a donkey engine burst into an irregular banging. Then the girl flared up. "I'll see him in hell first!"

He had never known her to swear before, even in running her mine, but he took it calmly. "Or, anyway, write him a note," he insisted doggedly.

"Certainly I won't write him a note!"

"Well . . . all right." Old Man Coffee got to his feet by means of jerks and hitches. "I first figured that maybe you'd want to make a signature on Curt's bail bond, but seems like they're not fixing to grant him any bail."

Mora Cameron looked blank. "Bail? What bail?"

Old Man Coffee returned her stare. His entire visit had

been spent in a state of slight bewilderment, but now he was openly astounded. Old Man Coffee had naturally assumed that Mora had heard the news, and for this he now cursed himself silently but with utter savagery. "I naturally supposed," he said humbly, "that you'd have been the first to hear!"

"If Curt's in jail," Mora said sharply, "I want to know. . . ."

"Child," said Coffee, "why, child, they're got Curt in jail on a charge of killing a man."

"Who was it?"

Old Man Coffee mumbled that he guessed it wasn't anybody that couldn't be spared. But somehow he knew she had already guessed the truth, that this had been no accidental killing, not even a fair stand-off fight, but—murder.

It was Art Dwyer, deputy sheriff, who had elected himself the victim, Old Man Coffee told her. There was no need to say who Art Dwyer was. Everybody had known the little, bowlegged deputy's hatchety face and permanent grin and tenacious political ambition.

This Art Dwyer had understood that a hot difference in views was on between Curt Morse and Dib Stalker. This was true. Dib Stalker was running a mine he called the Free Strike, right close to the Morse diggings. Due to lack of water, the Free Strike and the Morse Mine had to split a little flume trickle between them, and in this the two owners did not see eye to eye at all times. Lately Curt's black mood had run hard against Dib's stubbornness, and half of McTarnahan had expected something to explode. With unerring instinct for the wrong thing to do, the inspired Art Dwyer had gone busting up there to prevent a murder. And, instead, had joined right in the affair as the central figure.

"Come to cases," Mora said. She was watching him with wide, somber eyes that had gone from gray almost to black.

"Curt's own story is about all that's known," Old Man Coffee told her.

For one reason and another there were no witnesses, Dib Stalker and his foreman, Phil McGovern, in particular, having been conveniently far away. Curt claimed that it was just about dusk, and he was making some coffee, but being tired he dozed off in the shack. He was awakened by a shot. He went out. Art Dwyer's horse was stampeding down the gulch, and Art was lying three or four rods from Curt's door. A bullet had struck across the back of Art's neck, killing him instantly. The bullet had lost itself. Curt hadn't seen anybody around, and didn't have any theories. He had come down to McTarnahan at once to report.

They sat staring at each other until Old Man Coffee dropped his eyes. "Thin," Mora Cameron said faintly.

Old Man Coffee flipped her a startled glance. "Yes, thin," he agreed reluctantly. 'I thought maybe you'd want to go down."

Her voice faltered for the first time. "Tomorrow . . . tomorrow, maybe. I . . . I couldn't go down there now."

"Maybe a note, then?"

"I . . . all right."

She took a pencil and tried to write something on the back of an old blueprint. It took her a long time. Finally, with laborious effort, she got down two or three lines and handed the folded slip to the lion hunter.

Old Man Coffee brazenly unfolded that note, on the spot, and read it. All it said was:

Curt,
I don't hold it against you. If there is anything I can
do, let me know.

Mora

He hesitated. The note seemed to him so pitifully inadequate that he almost asked her to do it over, but he concluded that perhaps this was the best she could do. Mora was an inarticulate girl.

"I'll come up tomorrow," he told her, "if there's any news."

"All right."

But Old Man Coffee returned a little before midnight that same night. Mora was grave and quiet-faced, but he knew how shaky she was inside.

"There's something I forgot to tell you," he said. Mora Cameron was a tall, slim girl, straight as a lodgepole pine, but Old Man Coffee could still look down at her. And now he stood, glaring and tapping her collar bone with a horny forefinger like a tack hammer. "You know what?" he demanded at last. "Curt never killed that feller."

Mora sucked in a deep breath and for a moment seemed to sway, so that Old Man Coffee took hold of her arms. Then suddenly she angered. "Why didn't you say so . . . before I wrote that fool note? Curt will think I hadn't any belief in him!"

"Well," said Old Man Coffee, "well . . . heck!"

Mora stared, shy and tragic. "How . . . how did he take it? The note, I mean?"

Coffee hesitated. Down in the McTarnahan jail Curt Morse was just beginning to realize his danger, and was reacting to it in a way curiously suggestive of a dazed Newfoundland puppy. But Coffee was thinking of Curt's sudden whip-cut anger upon reception of Mora's note. The old hunter could see both sides—Mora's stunned inarticulacy, and the effect of bluntness and casual lack of faith that her note had conveyed to Curt. He lied. "How'd he take it? Not any special way."

Mora demanded distractedly: "How did you find out he didn't do it?"

"Hey, whoa! I never said I found out anything, child."

"But . . . you said Curt never killed. . . ."

"I took a look at the scene of the crime," he admitted, "and the only thing I got to base it on is . . . well, darn it! Curt let his coffee boil over." Old Man Coffee almost blushed. Never in his life had he had so little to go on—and that little so absurd.

"He let his . . . what?"

"I found where his coffee had boiled over on the stove. Now, suppose Curt had heard Art's horse coming up the trail. Suppose he said to himself . . . 'Here's a feller probably looking for trouble . . . I'll go out and give him some.' He would have had plenty of time to set his coffee off the fire, wouldn't he? And that's what makes me think it was like he says . . . he was dozing, and jumped up and run out when he heard the shot."

Probably never in his life had Old Man Coffee offered anyone so feeble a deduction. But Mora Cameron never questioned it. When she spoke again, she seemed to have quieted into a new cool energy, in the light of that slim glimmer of hope.

"Coffee," she said, "can you clear him?"

He deliberated. "I don't know. Given time. . . ."

"Time," Mora repeated. "Here . . . I'll tell you what. Tell Curt his friends have made up a pool . . . they're going to hire his counsel for him. Then you wire the best lawyers in the West. Get John Faversham and old Jim MacCready and Archer Smith. Especially, you've got to get Archer Smith."

Old Man Coffee stared at her. "You can't get no such men as that," he said. "I misdoubt if five thousand dollars will get old Jim MacCready's feet off his desk. At his age. . . ."

139

"Offer him ten, then. I'm telling you . . . get these men! If you need time, there's your time. Then . . . the rest is up to you. Put your nose on the trail! Everybody knows that you're the nearest thing to a human bloodhound the Frying Pan has ever seen."

"What else do you want me to do?" he said at last.

"Get Curt to name you to see that his mine is run."

"Who'll I get to run it?"

"Don't get anybody to run it. I'm going to run that mine!"

Art Dwyer was killed July 8th. And now the days went by and the weeks unrolled, and it was deep into August when one day Old Man Coffee plodded up the trail to the Morse Mine with a weary and springless stride. What Curt Morse did not know was that Mora Cameron was now making her headquarters at his diggings, to which she had transferred her entire force.

Today Coffee found her sitting on a dump car, watching the slow ram of the big stamp, and she turned to him quickly for the news that he now brought her every day.

"The prosecution is fighting for a quick trial, like a bobcat family in a barley sack," he said. "But your jackpot of lawyers fitted up their fourth delay this morning. It was either a Writ of Saleratus, or an Injunction to Deface. I never see the beat."

"How's Curt taking it?" Her attempted casualness fell through. With one thought, one emotion, forever uppermost in her mind, she should not have expected to fool Old Man Coffee.

"Quiet," Old Man Coffee stated. He didn't want to describe Curt's state of mind. Mora's poor, little, inarticulate note had had a sufficiently unfortunate effect. But when Curt had found that Mora was not even going to come to see him, he had gone utterly bitter, swearing that all women were alike. "Maybe you should have gone down there," Coffee suggested feebly.

"How could I? My only hope of winning through for him is never to let him suspect what I am doing, and only the hope of that is to treat him so . . . so badly . . . that he'll shut his ears to rumors."

Coffee nodded. "He don't suspect yet." He pushed ahead; he couldn't tell her that Curt's bitterness had long since trailed off into a hopeless funk in which Curt didn't seem to care whether he hanged or not. "Mora," he said, "I was wondering . . . them lawyers are wanting to know . . . how long we aim to keep on."

"Clear through to the end of the string. You could have told them that. What's the matter with you?"

Old Man Coffee looked savage, then dejected. "Mora," he said at last, "maybe I'm dumb. Maybe I don't know as much as I thought I did about the way folks act in a given case. But I've checked up on everybody who might have killed Art Dwyer . . . and I'm whupped."

Mora Cameron was silent for a long time. "And yet," she said at last, "and yet . . . Curt Morse never killed Art Dwyer." She turned on the old lion hunter abruptly. "You still believe that, don't you?"

He nodded. "To my dying day, I'll believe that Curt Morse never killed Art Dwyer."

"All right. You think you know where everybody was the night of the murder. But now we'll go back of that. We'll search the records of people long before this murder was done."

Old Man Coffee sat staring at her, very nearly aghast. "I wouldn't know where to commence," he said at last.

"I'll commence you, then," Mora told him. "We'll lead off with Dib Stalker that's been fighting with Curt over the flume water. Who was Dib Stalker before he came here? Where was he five years ago, and ten?"

"I don't know," said Old Man Coffee, "and, furthermore, I don't give a hoot. Any number of witnesses say that Dib Stalker was riding through McTarnahan when Art Dwyer was shot, and some of 'em I'd believe quicker'n I'd believe myself."

Mora showed impatience. "I know all that. We'll sift him anyway. And likewise his foreman, Phil McGovern."

"McGovern? Half an hour after the killing, Pete Crabtree himself saw Phil coming in with a fresh-shot deer that he'd got clear over on Bob Ridge. I've found the marks of blood where that deer. . . ."

"Sift him," Mora overrode him. "Go on from there and sift down those four others that were working at the Free Strike. . . ."

"And just how do you figure to do all this?"

"Get hold of the best national detective agency in the country. Get the two best in the country. Let them put on a dozen operatives apiece, and turn them loose."

"Now wa-it a minute," said Old Man Coffee. "Those birds will run fifty dollars a day expenses . . . apart from. . . ."

"Give them a hundred a day."

Old Man Coffee filled his pipe, then turned to her grimly. "You know what this case has been costing you?"

"Yes," said Mora.

"It'll cost you thousands more. And. . . ."

She turned on him, white with anger. "Move out . . . and make the wires smoke, before I. . . ."

Old Man Coffee moved out, and for another month the case dragged on.

For what seemed the thousandth time, Old Man Coffee

once more rode up the switchback trail to the Morse Mine to make his report to Mora. It was September, and the dejection of his attitude was subtly different now. The long strain was nearly over, ended in defeat. He hadn't enjoyed it. He was relaxed now, ready to accept an end to effort.

When he had found Mora, he paused a moment, marveling again at the staunchness with which this girl stood up under the long strain, courageously facing out inevitable defeat to the last ditch, to the last inch of ground.

"I was over at your mine," he said. "You've let it go plumb to ruin! It's all caved in and full of water."

Mora frowned. "If that's all you've got to talk about. . . ."

"There's one or two things I wanted to take up," Old Man Coffee admitted, "just by way of tying up the final loose ends."

The girl's breath sucked in. "Final?" she repeated.

"It's all washed up," he said doggedly. "And finished."

For a moment Mora Cameron seemed shaken. "We've got no case?"

"No, we got no case. Them lawyers think they could make a good showing if Curt would turn around and plead self-defense. But that's one thing he won't do."

"And Curt . . . what does he say?"

Coffee sought for words. A change had come over Curt Morse, so gradually that it had almost eluded the lion hunter. But lately Coffee had realized that Curt had found himself again, and in a new way. He had tempered and hardened, perhaps to an extent Coffee was unable to judge; the dazed, hopeless Newfoundland puppy was no longer in existence. "You know," he said slowly, "I believe that boy would fight now, given any chance."

"Then delay again," Mora ordered, the glow of tired fire burning in her eyes. "Delay and delay . . . you hear me?"

Old Man Coffee said gently: "We ain't ever going to have a case, Mora, looks to me. We got no place more to turn."

There was a silence, then Mora swung head and eyes right and left, like a cornered pony. "We haven't got the final report from that other detective agency yet."

"Yes, we have. It come in this morning."

"Nothing . . . nothing in it?"

"Nope. A little smidgen of something against Phil McGovern, of the Free Strike, some little thing he was charged with and run out on, up in Montana once."

She caught at that *little smidgen* like a trap closing on a falling leaf. "What was against him in Montana?"

"Oh, he flooded a mine, or something . . . sabotage, they called it. He jumped the state."

The starch seemed to go out of Mora. "Thin," she said.

"No good to us," Old Man Coffee agreed.

But Mora Cameron drew herself up. "It's little enough, God knows. But we'll use it."

"I don't see no connection," said Old Man Coffee.

"What connection do you need? We've found a flaw in the character of a man who hasn't been suspected yet."

"That don't bring him no nearer the scene of the crime."

Mora Cameron angered. "Someone was in this who proved he was not. Someone's alibi has got to be cracked. We'll bore through this stone wall yet, you hear me? But we'll never do it if we fail to drill and blast each least flaw! Go at Phil McGovern's alibi again," she was ordering him. "Shake down this deer-meat business. Comb the Bob Ridge country for anyone who heard a hunting rifle fired. Get Phil McGovern in the coop and go after him. Trick him out, and trap him, and don't be afraid to. . . ."

"Sheriff Crabtree . . . he won't fall in with no such. . . ."

"Good!" said Mora. "I've been waiting for a jam with

Sheriff Crabtree. I think he'll come to heel. But if he don't, we'll smash him clear out of the picture, if it takes my last cent!"

The old lion hunter groaned. "We can't do it, Mora," he said. "Phil McGovern is long gone from McTarnahan."

"Gone? McGovern gone?"

"These six weeks," Coffee told her.

"Why haven't you told me this before?"

"I can't report on the whole hooting population, Mora."

"Well, then . . . go get him!"

Old Man Coffee shook his head. "I've tried to locate which way he went. It's no go, Mora. Before we could lay hands on him, Curt Morse would be long hung."

Mora Cameron said nothing, and Old Man Coffee watched Curt Morse's big, antiquated rocker sway slowly, like a mechanical elephant, perhaps fifty or sixty times.

"You can't get McGovern?" Her eyes were wet, but they burned and glowed. "I'll show you how to get him!"

"Mora, girl, you gone nuts?"

"Get those operatives that traced down McGovern's history . . . they know his habits by now. Burn the wires with descriptions, cutting him off at the likely places first. But if it's necessary to post every crossroads on this continent, I'll foot the bill for that."

"You can't bring him back if you find him. Crabtree. . . ."

"To hell with Crabtree! I'm charging Phil McGovern with sabotaging in my mine. Nail him for that . . . and we'll see."

Old Man Coffee was appalled. Suddenly he turned on her and took hold of both her wrists. "Mora, you fool kid. . . ."

"Doing as I say," she demanded stubbornly, "can you get me Phil McGovern?"

Old Man Coffee gave up. "All right. I'll do it, Mora."

He started to turn away, but she stopped him. "One thing

more," she said, gathering control of her voice again. She picked up a scrap of board, and with a fragment of rock wrote down four or five figures, slowly, as if going over computations worked out before. She nailed the piece of wood onto the tailing dump. "For information leading to the arrest of Phil McGovern . . . thirty-five thousand dollars reward."

The old lion hunter nearly sat down flat. Weeks ago he had begun wondering where all the money was coming from. "Mora," he exploded, "thunderation! You're breaking yourself!"

"Look you here," Mora said. "One thing around here is dead certain . . . that I know how to take care of myself, first, last, and all the time. Get that through your head."

The thing dragged on again; September was nearly gone. Old Man Coffee didn't argue with her any more. He felt like a fool, carrying out her extravagant and futile orders, but he pursued them doggedly, to the letter. He had, however, devised a rough and practical alternative of his own. Failing to save Curt Morse's neck by legal means, Old Man Coffee felt impelled to rig up an illegal way. He had arranged for Curt Morse to break jail. For by this time Curt Morse was mentally in shape to carry out this rugged type of plan. The proposed jail delivery was waiting for nothing less obvious than the dark of the moon.

And then—without advance hope or warning, the whole case against Curt Morse collapsed, so quickly that even Old Man Coffee did not at first know what was happening. Art Dwyer had been killed on the 8th of July. On the 28th of September word came in over the wires that Phil McGovern was under arrest in Cheyenne, and on October 2nd Curt Morse walked out into the light of day.

McGovern had admitted nothing, and no one, least of all

Old Man Coffee, attached any significance to his arrest. But before Coffee could report to Mora, other things occurred that led him to withhold the news from her, lest he arouse false hope. Scouring his list of people who might have been on the prowl in that part of the country on or about the date of the murder, Old Man Coffee found a ranch cook who, like Phil McGovern, had been hunting, illegally, the week of the murder. Until now this man had seen no reason to shoot off his mouth at another's story, but he now admitted that he had seen the carcass of a buck hanging in a tree two miles back of the Free Strike. By searching his supplies purchased account, the cook was able to state definitely that he had observed the hung deer on the date of the killing of Art Dwyer.

Confronted with this new evidence, Mike Foley and Jack Hanson, double-jack men at the Free Strike, now admitted that they knew Phil McGovern to have killed his buck on the 7th and not the 8th. Returning to the Free Strike from his illegal hunt, Phil McGovern had seen a horse that he took to be the game warden's, so that he shied off, and cached his out-of-season kill until the next day.

Phil McGovern's alibi was destroyed. He was not as yet, however, connected with the murder either by motive or circumstantial implication. But now John Faversham proceeded to Lordstown and thence to Cheyenne by chartered plane. No one had ever questioned John Faversham's brilliance, his generalship, his resource. Yet McTarnahan was stunned—disbelieving—when, at the end of an all-night session at Cheyenne, he wired that Phil McGovern had confessed.

Even later, when it was revealed how Faversham had accomplished this, only those who had seen Faversham in action could imagine how the thing had been done. Faversham's approach to McGovern had assumed utter finality,

147

taking the view that only the just protection of McGovern himself required discussion. Starting with the disintegration of McGovern's deer-hunt alibi, Faversham built before the suspect's eyes a case complete in its presumptive detail, irresistible in its logic. Faversham's materials were slender—the failure of an alibi, and a forgotten charge of sabotage long ago. But he held one insuperable hidden advantage—his suspect's knowledge that the charge was true.

Perhaps it was McGovern's exact knowledge of his own guilt that caused him to perceive the closing jaws of a trap that did not exist. Perhaps the strain of the weeks at McTarnahan, while that old bloodhound Coffee had unceasingly snuffed and quartered so close to the true trail, had told upon McGovern beyond all measure. Perhaps, too, he was overawed by the power of talent arrayed in the defense of Curt Morse, so that he was glad now to accept Faversham's offer of assistance rather than face the merciless attack that they must unleash if McGovern elected to stand pat. In any case, the weight of the situation proved too much for Phil McGovern.

On October 1st John Faversham returned to McTarnahan with McGovern's detailed confession. By an understanding with Dib Stalker, McGovern was to have had a partnership in taking over the Morse Mine if Morse should be forced out of the picture. So, in the twilight of July 8th, McGovern had prowled the environs of the Morse Mine, looking for a chance to contribute to Curt's troubles. As Art Dwyer approached, McGovern had taken cover. Art's nervous horse had given away McGovern's presence. The deputy, perhaps hoping to shoot a bobcat, had drawn, turned his horse, and ridden directly upon Phil McGovern, who had gone into a panic and shot Art Dwyer down.

The gun with which Dwyer had been killed was found

where McGovern said he had thrown it, in a distant streambed. There were other conversations. Phil McGovern might or might not ultimately be convicted, but Curt Morse was clear.

Things had moved too fast for Old Man Coffee, making him realize that he was getting old. Even after Faversham's return to McTarnahan, the hunter was unable to overcome a skeptical disbelief in good fortune. It was not until the 2nd of October, the day of Curt's release, that Coffee finally brought himself to take the news to Mora.

He tried to think of some gentle yet dramatic approach— but he could not. "It's over with," he told her bluntly. "Curt Morse will be a free man within three or four hours."

Like himself, she was at first unable to comprehend. Little by little he fed her the details, clinching the circumstances one by one, until the whole sudden, preposterous story of the victory was complete.

"You've done it," he said. "Never in all my born days did I see the beat. That boy was a gone goose if ever a man was. And it was your fool, bull-headed persistence that drug him out. I never seen more silly and pointless moves than that last one you made. But it worked!"

"Luck," said Mora dully.

"Luck ain't no name for it," disagreed Old Man Coffee, "because no sensible person would ever have drawed near that luck."

Presently she said dully: "I'll have to pay off . . . pay off and get out. Well, it won't take long."

He sought for something to say. "I guess your own mine will be needing you bad for a while," he suggested.

She looked at him queerly. "I've got no mine."

"You . . . say, look here. . . ."

"I had to sell out to put up that last reward."

149

"Sell out? You couldn't sell! Caved and full of water. . . ."

"I know. But Sam Snowden . . . the old pirate, knew what it was. I had to take what he'd give . . . and like it."

"Why . . . girl! . . . you been lying to me? Why, you're bankrupt, then!"

"Yes," she said without expression, "I lied to you."

Old Man Coffee said explosively: "If I'd known . . . if I hadn't took your word. . . ." He stopped. In the face of the fact that her fanatic fight had, after all, pulled Curt Morse through, it was pointless to say that he would have prevented her. "He's wanting to see you now," he said gently at last.

"See him? I can't ever see him!"

"You can't see. . . . Hey! What's this, now?"

"Don't you see?" The words came out of her in a rush. "I can't help it if I'm a miner. I can't help it if things make it look like I'm a better miner than he is. I suppose I'll always be a miner. And he hates me for it. It isn't fair . . . but it's true!"

"Any pup in the world would be grateful for. . . ."

"Grateful!" Mora flared up wildly. "Who wants gratitude? Don't you see how much worse it is now? When he finds out that I've run his mine . . . and I've run it well! . . . and finds out where the money came from that brought the lawyers, and ran down McGovern. . . ."

"If that pup has the guts to look cross-eyed. . . ."

Mora cried out crazily: "It isn't that! But down in the bottom of his heart he'll always hold it against me. If ever he made love to me again, I'd feel . . . *I'd feel as if I had bought him*. I couldn't stand it! I couldn't!"

"Mora," said Old Man Coffee stubbornly, "you got to see him anyhow."

Mora came to her feet like a jumped deer. "I won't! I won't never! I'll be out of here in an hour, and after that this country can't hold me any more. And if you try to follow me, or help him follow me, you old ground owl. . . ."

Old Man Coffee looked upset. "I guess I might's well show down my hand," he decided. He stepped to the door and shouted down trail: "Hey, Curt! Curt, come up here!"

Mora went white. "What . . . ?"

"I made him wait down there behind the tailings until I could break the news," Old Man Coffee was explaining. "I didn't want to scare you, like seeing a ghost. He . . . he knows, Mora. I told him about what you've done."

The girl's eyes looked enormous in her white face, and her hands were pressed to her temples.

Curt Morse stood in the doorway of his shack, hands in pockets, making it look as if it were cut for a smaller race. The months he had spent out of the sun had not changed the fact that he was strapping big, with rocky shoulders fit to step off under a 500-pound pack.

His back was to the light so that Old Man Coffee could not see the expression on his face. But he could see Mora's face, and it was full of white panic. In spite of her field boots and rough dungarees he had never seen her look so slim and fragile, or so out of place in that gaunt, harsh-edged background.

"Let me by!" Mora cried out in a smothered voice. "I . . . want to get out of here!"

Curt Morse said: "Now, shucks; I don't know as you do." He was grinning a little, but gently and sorrowfully. And now Old Man Coffee saw what perhaps he should have seen before—that all the black bitterness and pride had gone out of the youngster, and the hardness that had come into him was a fine kind of hardness, letting his brain work again in a new and better way. Old Man Coffee was looking at a mining man.

"You don't want to go any place," Curt said.

Suddenly Mora's spirit seemed to buckle and collapse altogether. Tears flooded her cheeks, and she hid her face in her hands.

Curt Morse said: "Shucks, now." He stepped forward and picked her up, cradling her in his arms as if she were a child.

Man with a Future

The last man to run was the company doctor—not because he was any braver than the rest, but because he was a terrific sleeper. He did not hear the shouts of fire, or the bosses' bellowing, or the stampeding of the 400 men. He would have slept through it all, perhaps on into eternity itself, if a muleskinner named Bill Something had not come back to wake him up.

Once awake, the good doctor made excellent time up the mountain. He ran with a sort of cool fervor, calculating as he ran just how far and fast he would have to climb to escape being assisted by the coming dynamite blast. He finally collapsed behind a forty-ton block of granite about a quarter mile above the camp, blowing magnificently. As soon as he could breathe without seeing stars, he crawled to the corner of the granite block and looked back. The night was a dark one, and nowhere blacker than in the deep cut of Cinnebar Gulch. In that blackness the long, racing arms of the brush fire ran like rivers of the forest's red-gold light.

Luckily the brush grew only in the bottom of the gulch; the high-piled black rock on the mountainside was bare. The danger derived from the four tons of dynamite that, by an act of utter folly, was stacked under a tarpaulin at the upper end of the camp. Dynamite in that quantity is supposed to be stored with the utmost care, but this time, through a slight error, it had been hauled in before the storehouse was dug.

The doctor seriously considered climbing higher, but little time was left for climbing. The gulch was drawing the fire up like a chimney. As he watched, the first tents caught and went up in flames, burning nicely. The flanking arms of the fire had reached the full length of the partly cleared camp. Already they were on either side of that insanely placed dynamite. He could see the square block of dynamite cases plainly, its tarpaulin-covered sides gleaming, clear-cut in the golden light.

Right then the doctor made a sudden strangling noise, and his chin hit his knees, and his eyes popped, for he saw the man. The man was standing on the dynamite itself, sprinkling about him with a slender line of hose from the water tank. Even at that distance there was no mistaking the immensely long stilt legs, and the awkward, lurching stride of that fellow, stepping around on top of the dynamite cases. It was the muleskinner named Bill.

The doctor's voice burst out of him in a hysterical, futile shout: "Bill! For God's sake . . . !"

He stopped shouting. The brush fire was booming and roaring like the surf of a sea in hell. Bill could not have heard if the doctor had been shouting in his ear.

But now a pair of hands grabbed the doctor, startling him so that he almost fell off the mountain. "What is it? What's the matter?"

The number two refugee behind the granite block was a girl. Her name was Caroline Schultz, and she was the daughter of one of the hard-rock bosses.

"There's a man down there!" the doctor gabbled. "Some blockhead is trying to save the dynamite!"

She crowded closely to look around the rock. He saw her mouth twist open as if she were going to scream, except that she did not. Then the doctor made a wild snatch and caught her wrist just as she dodged around him.

"You can't go down there!" He braced against the rock and pulled.

"Let me go," the girl whimpered. "I've got to get him out of there!"

"Not a chance! That stuff lets go any second now!"

She gave up then, beginning to cry, and he let her look down at the camp again. The smoke was rolling over Bill in heavy waves, but they could see that he was still on his feet. Sometimes they could see the red flash of the water he threw.

The girl subsided into the doctor's arms. She said: "It's my fault. He wouldn't be down there, except for me. He's followed me everywhere I've been for the last two years."

The doctor pulled the girl down behind the rock. They sat there, then, and waited. They waited a long time.

Strangely nothing happened. When at last they looked again, they saw that the worst of the fire had swept on up the gulch. A big piece of burning brush whisked upward on a puff of breeze and tumbled to rest up against the dynamite. They saw Bill take two long, lazy strides and kick it away. Then they stopped breathing again. Nonchalantly, casually Bill was stamping out the sparks! The big, swinging wallops of the high-heeled boots looked as if he were determined to blow up, even yet.

Now a few of the tougher of the hard-rock men were moving back in, running clumsily through the hot ashes in their heavy boots. Some of them joined Bill on top of the dynamite and made him stop that stamping around. In another five minutes they had a bucket brigade going, damping out the edges of the tarpaulin where it had dried and begun smoldering in the heat. Presently, when the girl started down the mountain again, the doctor let her go.

The doctor followed more slowly. A dazed, flabbergasted, but admiring crowd was banked around Bill. Caroline was in Bill's arms, crying on his scorched shirt and hanging onto him as if she would never let him go.

The doctor pried her loose. A couple of the cook tents were still standing, and the doctor dragged Bill into one of these, laid him out on a table, and began smearing him with lard. He was thinking sentimentally that Bill had a future yet. A man with Bill's courage, and the devotion of a girl like Caroline, would surely. . . .

"If I'd 'a' knowed it was fixing to get so hot," Bill said, "I wouldn't've stayed. I never been so discommoded in my life."

"You're sure the hero around here now," the doctor told him.

"I oughta be," Bill agreed. "The whole darn' camp would shore be going hungry if it wasn't for me. That pile of grub would have gone up like tissue paper. You realize it takes four days to haul grub from. . . ."

"Grub? What grub?"

"That pile of grub under the tarpaulin."

The doctor stood back and looked at him. "Bill," said the doctor, "don't you ever breathe this to a living soul. You just sit back and take the credit as it comes. But there wasn't any grub under that tarpaulin, Bill."

"Huh?"

"That's a sack of dynamite cases, and. . . ."

There was a faint bleat, and the doctor's voice trailed off. The hero of Cinnabar Gulch had fainted cold.

Old Thunder Pumper

Ordinarily good luck stuck just as close to Mississippi Tyler as did that big foolish hound of his that was the laughingstock of the rim-rock country. But, now that he needed it more than he ever had in his life, that luck seemed to peter out, having only the ubiquitous hound for solace—and the hound, of course, was useless.

It was a funny thing about Mississippi's luck. It had first picked him up when he had come to the Southwest ten years before, at the age of fourteen. Just as a sample—he had been tricked into paying five dollars for a three-year-old pony that had a bowed tendon, and hence was worthless, but the tendon turned out to be merely sprained, and, when it was well, the pony proved one of the fastest in the Arizona rim rock, and Mississippi sold him for $500.

The luck was still holding three years later, when he sent back to Mississippi for a pack of red-bone hounds and became a lion hunter. Mountain lions drew a bounty of $100 a head, put up by the rim-rock ranchers, wolves the same, bears the same, with an added $100 for each bear pelt. In the first month of his hunting he went after a deep-cañon silvertip that had bluffed the best hunters of the rim rock and at the very first stab walked into—not one bear, but two together, that stood looking at him out of a berry patch—and on the way home his dogs treed a mountain lion, making it a $500 day. Things like that, always, throughout the whole of his ten years in the Southwest.

Old Gar Brent was the barrier against which Mississippi's luck broke. You couldn't do much with Gar Brent, because the old man had a weak heart, and an attack was likely to come on him at any time. An attack was on him now, as Mississippi stood, hat in hand, in the Brent cabin, with that big, worthless hound of his peering out from behind his legs.

Willa Brent, old Gar's daughter, was fussing around her father, her slender, capable hands tucking a blanket around Brent's knees, and offering him hot water and soda.

"My time's come . . . this time . . . ," old Brent gasped out. No question about it, his breath was mighty labored, and there was nothing natural about the flesh over his cheek bones or the peculiar glassy brightness of his eyes. "Played out my string . . . this time . . . for sure. . . ."

Mississippi Tyler, who had heard Brent say the same thing perhaps ten or a dozen times before, was unimpressed. He had a theory that if Gar Brent would lay off the overeating. . . .

But Willa took it pretty hard, which was usual, too. She really believed that her father was going to die one of these times and always took the latest attack for the fatal one. What Mississippi was noticing was how lovely Willa looked, her eyes so big and dark in her white face. He felt like choking old Brent for scaring her so.

"Shut up them damned dogs!" Brent ordered.

Mississippi's good pack of red-bone hounds was making considerable noise all right. There were twelve of them, of a fox-hound size and look, but with coon-dog in them, too, so that they were of all colors from solid black to pinto. It was almost comical how little it took to set them yelling; they all belled effortlessly, from any position and at the least excuse.

Willa shot Mississippi a compassionate look as he went to the door and told the dogs to shut up—he'd be out in a minute. It pleased him that Willa had a liking for those hound voices. He didn't know, though—and if he had, it would have surprised him—quite how much Willa did love the belling of those dogs or how often she had listened for the first sound of them, off over the range, musically sending word downwind that Mississippi was on the way.

"What's that mutt doing in here?" rasped Brent pettishly, his eye falling on the big worthless one at Mississippi's knee.

Mississippi Tyler had long been aware that Brent disliked dogs in general, and this one in particular, but Brent had never before come right out and insulted the dog.

"Go outside, Pumps," said Mississippi apologetically. The dog went out, and in a minute they could hear the animal muttering to himself in deep bass tones, like no other hound. The sound seemed to annoy Gar Brent out of all reason.

"The Thunder Pumper," sneered Brent irrationally. "The Thunder Pumper! Pumping noise is all he's good for. I know all about him. He's never treed a lion yet, nor stood a bear, and he eats for three! A good sample of Mississippi worthlessness is what he is!"

"Dad, be quiet . . . rest yourself," Willa remarked.

Mississippi reddened. Not many things ever angered him, but this did because it was true, and no one knew it better than he. The Thunder Pumper had been sent him by mistake along with some others, and he was certainly too slow for lion work. When the pack took a hot trail, running full cry, the Thunder Pumper could be found miles to the rear, baying each individual track after a close, conscientious inspection. *Sniff, sniff . . . he set foot exactly here. Bloo-oop! Sniff . . . here is his next step. No, wait. Yes, I am sure. Bluh . . . wowp!*

Like as not the pack would tree the lion, and Mississippi— himself left far behind, but riding as hard as was practical in that deep-cleft country of the Mogollon—would come up and shoot the lion, and skin it, and the dogs would eat it. Then, five or six miles down the trail, they would perhaps meet the Thunder Pumper, still painstakingly baying out the trail of that lion that was already out of this world and digested. And unless pulled off the trail by force, he was quite likely to walk right on through the returning pack, oblivious to everything but the trail beneath his nose.

Yet Mississippi had a deep, understanding love for that huge, useless dog with the homely, sorrowful face and trailing ten-inch ears. Perhaps because Mississippi always looked a little like a misfit himself.

As he stood in Brent's cabin there was white Southwestern dust all over him—alkali on his worn neckerchief, on his broad, slouch-brimmed hat, on the fancy stitching of his high-heeled boots. He loomed mighty big, loose-jointed, and kind of lazy-looking, like a true Westerner. But in his sun-whipped blue eyes was always a lazy laughter, the laughter of another country mellower than rim rock and desert, a country where mild, gentle river vapors take the edge off the sun and draw blue songs out of brown water.

Up levee, down levee, Mississippi water
Brown water, high water, back water slack

The syncopated rhythms of the Mississippi bottoms breathed out of him, and, as soon as you heard him singing blues to himself, you knew at once why this man looked out of place, that here was a big hunk of Mississippi a thousand miles away from home and the mud not dry.

"This is the end of me," said Gar Brent again, fixing glassy eyes on his daughter.

"Maybe in the morning . . . ," suggested Mississippi politely.

"I've just got two requests," said Gar Brent, disregarding him. "Willa, git me that box there, under my bunk."

"Requests?" echoed Mississippi. "From whom?"

"Requests to make!" Gar Brent snapped. From the shoe box of odds and ends that Willa had brought him he rummaged forth a sealed letter. "This here is to your second cousin at Red Stick. If I put in my chips, promise you'll send this to him."

"I promise," whispered Willa.

"That's Henery Brent, the widowed fellow with the five young kids?" Mississippi inquired. He was disregarded again.

"My will is in that, and my instructions," said Gar Brent. "Henery is to work this horse ranch for you, and hold it in trust until you're thirty-one years old."

"Don't you mean twenty-one, Mister Brent?" Mississippi offered.

"Thirty-one, I said!" Gar Brent paused to catch up with his laboring breath, and glared at Mississippi Tyler, then at the Thunder Pumper, who had sneaked back in and once more regarded Brent with dolorous interest, from behind Tyler's legs.

"I got one other last request," Brent went on. "I know that what you promise, Willa, that you'll do. I know I can depend on that. From here out, I want you to have nothing more to do with this Mississippi Tyler."

There was a moment's struck silence, while the labored breathing of Gar Brent continued regularly. Then Willa said slowly, her voice low: "Why, Dad . . . ?"

"This," said Gar Brent, "is the last thing I'll ever be asking of you. It's for your own good, and you owe me that much, Willa, if only so's I can die in peace."

"But . . . ," began Willa, her voice queer, and stopped.

"I reckon," said Mississippi, "I'll be going now. Don't answer him yet, Willa. I don't want to hear this, I guess."

"Wait, Mississippi," said the girl.

"You hadn't ought to ask me," said Tyler. "The Tylers

live forever, and I don't want to be remembering your answer
to that, all the long way."

"*Moo-woh,*" commented the Thunder Pumper in a dolorous moan.

"Shut up, Pumps!"

"Take that dog out and shoot it!" snarled Gar Brent.

"Pardon me, Mister Brent?"

"If you think I'm joking, I'll put it like this," said the
strained voice of the old man, "shoot that damned worthless
hound, and I'll take my request back!"

"That's ridiculous, Mister Brent."

"It ain't the dog," said Brent, "so much as the principle of
the thing. It's a test, to see if you can choose between Willa
and your own worthless ways."

"It's a plumb tyrannical old whim," said Mississippi,
"and, even if it wasn't, I wouldn't have anything to do with
it."

"If you like that dog better than Willa, that's up to you."

"But," the girl put in, her eyes dark with an unreadable
emotion, "if he'll get rid of Pumps some other way. . . ."

"No," Mississippi supplied, "I'm not going to get rid of
Pumps, not in any way at all." It did not occur to him that there
was any choice about it. "Now, if you'll excuse me, I'll go."

"And you don't need . . ."—the raving voice of Gar Brent
followed him—"you don't need to come back! Worthless . . .
Mississippi hound-pusher. . . ."

When Mississippi Tyler had mounted, however, he de-
layed a bit. The little half-broke mustang on which he sat kept
jigging and skittering sideways, anxious to be gone; only Tyler's easy-going, good-natured hands, that automatically
took half the tangle out of any horse he mounted, made it possible to manage the animal at all. But Mississippi held him in,
and waited.

He had a hunch that Willa was going to come out and speak to him, never noticing the pony's plunge as again he stepped clear, and, when he saw that Willa Brent's lips were quivering and that her eyes were full of tears, he took a step toward her to pick her up in his arms. But, for some reason, he did not.

"I'm sorry, Mississip'. I've liked you . . . a lot. I guess you know."

He waited.

"I guess I'll have to ask you not to come here any more, though, now."

"He's not dying," Tyler said. He had known that Willa would feel that it was to her father that she owed the first debt, but it came hard just the same. "He's not dying any more than I am," he said again. "But I'll do like you say." He turned suddenly and brought down the head of the pony with such a heavy hand that for a moment the little beast stood motionless, in sheer amazement, while he mounted.

"I'll tell you this," said Mississippi slowly, with the nervous pony shifting back and forth under him. "Someday you're going to come looking for me, Willa. God grant us I be there, that's all."

"Never!" she cried furiously. "Not if you were the last man in the world!"

Back in his cabin above the Mogollon Rim he remembered that, and believed it, too, and he wondered what had ailed him, that he should have said what he did. The setting sun was striking redly through the door of his cabin, and by its light he looked about him curiously, as if he were just coming out of a strange place.

Slowly he packed his mule. Then he rummaged in his traps until he found an old rusty padlock and hasp, which had somehow come with the other stuff from Mississippi, and with this he locked the door. That was something else that was new in the rim rock, for a man to lock his door.

"L-i-on-n-n!" he told the dogs. They always answered when you spoke to them in certain tones, and, although he had heard that absurdly unanimous chorus answer his voice thousands of times, it always tickled him, and made him smile. He smiled now. "Time to move on," he told them, setting loose those hair-trigger bell voices again.

The key to the cabin he threw into Rustler's Gulch.

He had no way of knowing that Gar Brent died that night, actually pushing in his chips at last, after all those false alarms.

Mississippi was gone a month. His hunting did not take him more than a few days' ride from his cabin, but he did not return to it. Although no misfortune of a positive nature overtook him, it was one of the most luckless and vacant months he had ever known.

The red-bone pack picked up no sign of lion or bear. Sometimes the pack bayed a hot trail, but Mississippi could tell by their voices what the quarry was, and each time he pulled them off some trail of no worth.

Bob and Flora disgraced themselves by crying—"Bear!"— for nine miles, at the end of which they surrounded a porcupine. And young Three led the whole pack into five sight-runnings after deer—the worst outrage a trail pack can descend to, since it leads to ruination of their usefulness.

The end of the month found Mississippi dirty, bearded, and in morose temper. He had carried a picture of Willa Brent's face in his mind ever since he had first seen her, three years before, and it had cast a glow over the commonplaces of his rigorous life. But now he was trying to shut that picture out, and the light was gone out of the rim rock. He was just another of those men who are tougher than lobos in the face of male opposition or hardship, but somehow can be downed without a struggle by a woman's adverse word. He didn't care much any more whether the pack spoiled itself or not.

Then one night, as he called in his dogs, the long trombone blast of the cow horn he used was answered by signal shots a couple of miles away, and, by the time he had lit his fire, he was joined by Clem Harky, an old acquaintance of the Lazy Y outfit.

"Right glad to see you, boy," Mississippi told him. "I. . . ." He paused suddenly, for, as the rider came into the firelight, Mississippi saw that he was haggard and weary. "What's bust?" he demanded.

"You ain't heard?" said Harky.

"How would I?" growled Mississippi. "I suppose I've seen two men in a month."

"Willa Brent's lost."

"Lost? What do you mean? *How* lost?"

"She's missing a week already . . . today."

"What . . . how . . . where was she seen last?" Mississippi finally got out.

Harky squatted on his heels and filled one cheek with Copenhagen snuff, before, with his eyes on the fire, he answered slowly, seeming to test his words: "A week ago today I seen her riding up that Mogollon trail toward your cabin. She was too fur to speak, but I waved, and she waved back. That night I rode over to see her. She never come home." He paused uneasily, as if he realized that he had linked Mississippi with the disappearance in a way he did not intend. But in a moment he went on: "I waited for her at the Brents', and, seeing she didn't come in, I took the up trail about three in the morning. I got to your shack about six. The fresh tracks of her pony was there. But the door was locked. She hadn't been in. I followed on down her trail. Afterward, it seemed like to me she had been following the old trail of your horse and mule, but I didn't think nothing about it then. Willa's slept out before. There wasn't anything 'specially peculiar about it. Only, being interested in her, kind of, I followed along to make sure she was all right.

"By and by, I begun to worry, and pressed along pretty hard. So before night I come on her night camp. She seemed to have shot something to eat. They'd told me, back at her house, she didn't have any grub along. Next day, early, I found her pony in Cross Cañon. He'd fell and busted a leg, and she'd shot him through the head. I'd have supposed she'd turn back, but, instead, she'd walked on."

Mississippi was counting back. "That would have been about last Tuesday," he computed. "Why . . . I was within two miles of Cross Cañon that morning!"

"That maybe accounts for her walking on," said Harky, talking to the fire. "Heard your hounds, likely, and hoped to borry an animal to go back on. Did she signal you, that you know of?"

"I heard shots, over thataway . . . thought it was somebody hunting," said Mississippi in a strained voice.

"And then . . . well, now that you mention being over there, it looks like she'd just kind of followed you on. . . ."

"Oh, good God!" burst out Mississippi. He remembered that he had worked all up and down and across that ragged and forbidding country of pine and broken granite, and he could imagine how often Willa had heard his hounds, sometimes near, then presently far away again, taunting her like a will-o'-the-wisp of sound.

"I managed to work out the trail to within a few miles of Crackman's Rocky before I lost it in the rocks. The trail had got kind of wandering and uncertain by then, like as if she wasn't going to be able to go on much more. Mississip', we've combed the Crackman country with a currycomb since then. There's been about twenty fellows searching the last few days. We've hallooed and fired off guns fit to raise the dead. It's a wonder you didn't hear."

"I've been working a long ways beyond the crest," Mississippi told him. "I was only near Cross Cañon a day and a half. You'd have heard me as easy as I would have heard you, I guess, the way the dogs moan out."

"But she's disappeared into thin air," Harky concluded. "Today I heard your dogs coming nearer all day, and I rode to meet you, to see if maybe you'd picked her up, or knew of her. Or else . . . I thought we might give the dogs a try at following her across Crackman's Rocky."

"We're starting now," said Mississippi. "My pony can keep on a little more, I guess. It'll be fifteen, eighteen miles."

When Mississippi had saddled, he whacked off a couple of long strips of yesterday's venison roast and gave Clem Harky one. The rest of the haunch he left behind with the dogs, knowing that when they had finished they would follow.

"I can't figure why on earth she should take it into her head. . . ."

"Can't say I blame her much for running out," said Harky, his voice flat and hard with fatigue. "Ever since Gar Brent died. . . ."

"Since Gar Brent *what?*"

"You didn't know her paw was dead? Why, you was there the afternoon he was took!"

"I supposed it was just another of those cry-wolf conniptions."

"Yeah, that's what any of us would've thought. Well, she sent a letter he'd writ to her second cousin at Red Stick, and Gar hadn't been buried a week when this Henery Brent moved in on her with his five kids. Quite a heap of washing and cooking to come down on a girl, all in a lump. And Henery, he put me in mind of a half-breed Paiute the way he just sat around watching her work, and wearing out his pants. And, Mississip' boy, them hell-raising kids! Still, she told me she was going to be able to stick it, providing he cut out making love."

"Making love?"

"Kind of peculiar position a second cousin is in. He's blood kin enough so's he can move in his family without causing talk, especially since it was at the request of her paw, yet from another angle he ain't so much blood kin as to keep him from getting pretty fresh romantic. I could see how she might get smoked out of house and home, all right."

"And me gone hunting," Mississippi almost wept. "I should have kept better track, Clem. Only . . . her paw made her promise she wouldn't have anything to do with me. I should be shot for paying any attention to it."

"Yeah, you should," Clem monotoned. "Everybody knew Willa was right sweet on you, Mississip'. Everybody but you, anyway. . . . And now that she's got herself lost, come looking for you. . . ."

"For God's sake, shut your mouth!"

Just before dawn they pulled up and waited for the light, and, when it came, Clem Harky sighted in his landmarks and located the dim, inconspicuous print of a small heel.

"That's the last earthly sign, Mississipp'."

Mississippi Tyler got down and brought his dogs about him. He hardly knew how to put them onto this new kind of trail. He made them all lie down, then took Chicoree by the scruff.

"This is it," he told the red and white leader, making his

voice exciting. He pushed the dog's nose hard down on the track. "Get it, and like it, and hang on! Now, go on!"

In all that red-bone pack Chicoree was the brains. Mississippi feared he would not get the idea, since the method was new, but Chicoree did. The trail was old, considering the dry heat of the hill, but Chicoree's voice blared, and he got off at a trot.

Holding the rest in was hard, but Mississippi managed it with voice and quirt, forcing their noses to the heel print, one after another. Most of them would have taken the cue from Chicoree, but he wanted to be sure. Last of all, the Thunder Pumper volunteered and gravely examined the heel print as the others had been forced to do.

They pressed forward briskly for a little while, for here the trail was on fairly favorable ground, compared to what was ahead. And presently, searching the tough soil with their eyes, the men found another visible print that the way of the dogs had shown.

"They've got it," Harky exulted. "By God, they know their work!"

"Don't cheer yet," said Mississippi.

"You're thinking of Crackman's Rocky!"

"That, and something else." You see, they did not know what would be at the end of that trail, even if it was ever reached.

Roy Lindstrom joined them presently, guided to them by the clamor of the pack. He reported that there was no news. "Never seen such a disappearance as this," Lindstrom admitted. "I've been in the rim rock near forty years, and thought I knew it pretty good, but this beats me."

"We'll be to the end soon now," said Clem.

Mississippi told them they had better not get up their hopes. Ahead loomed the far-stretching, crack-laced granite surfaces of the mesa called Crackman's Rocky. It lay low in the desert, that vast, ancient pour of rock. It had been a molten flow once, but the ages had split and broken its surfaces with 10,000 clefts. On the one hand Crackman's Rocky lost itself in the desert sands that buried it, and on the other surged into the abrupt lofty ledges of the Mogollon Rim, along which it lay mile on mile. Mississippi had been dreading the arrival of the hounds at Crackman's Rocky and hoping the trail would skirt it, for granite forever baked in the Southwestern sun holds but little scent—and that for not very long.

Up the slope of the granite Chicoree led the pack, and by the leader's instant voice change Mississippi knew that the granite told them nothing. The dogs were running on general direction and hope. After a few hundred yards Chicoree admitted it and back-cast to the sand, but once more upon the granite lost his way. Casting carefully, checking both sides of the widening dike to see that the trail did not leave, Chicoree led them on until at length they came to a widening of those naked long reaches of stone, and Mississippi dismounted. Somberly he loosened his cinches and sat down on a block of rock.

"We'll be here some little time," he told the other two slowly. "There's nothing to do now but wait."

A long time passed without result. Once Chicoree voiced uncertainty, and the pack rallied to him full cry, but it came to nothing, and Chicoree later denied his own belief.

Every hound pack has a dog that is both bully and trail expert—boss in every way. If a man is said to have a crack lion pack, it usually boils down to one leader. In Mississippi's pack Chicoree was that one best dog, a time-sharpened, red-and-white hound that was seldom still, but used his head just the same. Often, when the pack had lost a cold trail, and were fanned out twelve ways in futile casting, Mississippi had seen Chicoree standing, silent and alone, pretending to test the empty wind. Then presently Chicoree would go trotting off some new way, up a draw, perhaps, that the trail had not suggested, and in another quarter of an hour would come his jubilant belling, sometimes from far away: *Lion! Lion!* Then all the pack would swing in on the recovered trail, and they would run that lion down. So, with the trail lost on the hot naked rock, it was Chicoree upon whom Mississippi depended.

"I've combed this throw of the rock twenty times," complained Harky. "I found out as much as the dogs did . . . with my own eyes. If this is the best they can do, we might as well. . . ."

"Give him time," said Mississippi. "Chicoree's left the pack, and gone off on his own. You'll hear him, pretty soon now. There's a *hound* dog. I don't suppose he'd been stumped three times in as many years. Give him a chance!"

Yet an hour passed, and two hours. The pack was becoming impatient and discouraged. Those that had cast wide were coming in, waiting for Chicoree's voice. Chicoree might strike the trail beyond the earshot of the men, but the hounds would hear and answer, following him up—once he belled.

Then, at the end of three hours, Chicoree came in. He carried his head and tail low, a foolish-looking, red and white form that was for once completely silent. That old war dog, that had made all the hunting reputation Mississippi had, had met utter defeat, and knew it, and was done.

Mississippi sat down for a moment, his face in his hands. Clem Harky and Roy Lindstrom were silent, tired men on tired mounts. No one knew the rim rock better than these three, but now they did not know where to go that they had not already gone, or which way to turn. About Mississippi began to gather the weaker hounds, half a dozen that flopped down around him in rag-like postures, plainly considering the hunt ended.

Chicoree was still casting, or pretending to, at a disconsolate walk, and so were Belle and Strap, and the two pups, Three Star and Hennessy, were still running in their perpetual circles, making a big show of remembering what they were after, which probably they did not. And of course there still kept coming to them the deep bass *bloomps* of the Thunder Pumper, coming up so slowly that he was still working that part of the trail that was on favorable earth. But all that had no meaning, with Chicoree beat. And as the hours passed, it was easy to see the pack was demoralized.

"It's getting late," said Linstrom.

Mississippi rose, his face grim and gray as the face of the baffling rock itself. Slowly he tightened his cinch. "They may pick it up some other place," he offered without conviction. "We'll swing some long circles of our own, using our heads the best we can."

Mississippi stuck a foot in the stirrup, but there, suddenly, he checked. "Wait a minute," he said in a queer voice.

He had cast one glance back along the way they had come, and something he had glimpsed there held him immobile. The two other riders followed his eyes.

Then, through a break in a split ledge, appeared a slow, low-headed form, so far off and so formlessly gray against gray that they could hardly make out what it was—until it lifted its head and the deep halloo of the Thunder Pumper came up the wind.

"Aw, it's only . . . ," began Clem Harky.

"He can't do nothing," grunted Linstrom.

Mississippi's voice was hardly audible, but it seemed torn

out of him, so that it cut down the comments of the others. "Pumps is on the rock!"

"You mean he's . . . ?"

"Wait!"

They could see the Thunder Pumper more plainly now, a putty-colored, splay-footed, big-pawed dog, his long ears dragging on the rock. At every other step he paused to sniff deliberately, and each time he bayed before he passed on. *Sniff-sniff . . . she set foot here. Blooroop! . . . and here, again. No, wait. Yes, I am sure. Bloowowup! And the next step was here. . . .*

Slow, deadly slow, baying individually each invisible print, the Thunder Pumper came on. He was working just as he had always worked the scent of lions, on all those long trails whose ends he had reached futilely, after the quarry was long dead. Faithful to himself—that was it, loyal first and always to the convictions that were bred in his blood and bone.

Slowly it dawned on Mississippi that the Thumper Pumper did not know that he had come to barren rock where no scent could hold, that he was not aware that he was working a vanished trail that no dog nose could hope to detect. For to the Thumper Pumper all difficulties and all trails had at last proved the same, and he was working the vanished scent exactly as he had worked his first hot, reeking bear track a long time ago.

Bloowump. Awump, awump! Here she stepped, I know. And here . . . let us make certain. Yes, exactly here. Wowooo-oh! Pumping doleful thunder over every lost touch of Willa Brent's boot.

"Can it be possible he knows . . . ?"

"You bet he knows," said Mississippi, the muscles tight around his eyes. "Slow, ghastly slow, always, but wrong? He never was wrong in his life. . . ."

The tears were running down Mississippi's leather face by now. That was partly for love of that slow, honest dog that had been true to his own ways all these years to serve his purpose here. But mostly because the beloved trail the Thunder Pumper traced was a broken, wavering line. *She . . . was looking for me,* he told himself over and over. *I'm never going to forgive myself for that.*

Then—the Thunder Pumper faltered. He had come to the place where a brace of hounds had laid their hot, smoking bodies on the rock, and all over the stone, too, were the invisible trampling trails the twelve dogs had made, and the men, and the horses' musky-smelling hoofs. He stopped and lifted his head, and for the first time slowly turned to look Mississippi in the face with his mournful yellow eyes. It was as if he said: *This is as far as I can go . . . there is no more left. . . .*

Mississippi did not speak, because he could not. Slowly he sat down, and averted his face from the other men. The Thunder Pumper whimpered—and put down his head. And once more he was lost in the mysteries of the trail.

At sunset the Thunder Pumper brought them to the edge of the rock, still step by step to the last; here the red-bone pack—the pack that had failed—recognized the trail shown to them on the better earth. The horses could no longer keep up, and Mississippi followed the dogs alone at a stumbling run through the starlight.

So finally he came to a limp, slender figure lying, motionless, in a ravine, not ten yards from a point at which Clem Harky had passed in his hallooing search. Although a dozen had ridden there, they would hardly have found her, so still did she lie under the chinquapin scrub. She was alive. . . .

Before Willa Brent at last opened her eyes and knew where

she was, or with whom, she was established in Mississippi's bunk, in the cabin he had built thinking of her.

"Will you ever forgive me, Mississippi?"

"For what?"

"For coming here. . . ."

"Why, honey child. . . ."

"I just couldn't stand it any longer, Mississippi."

"It must have been terrible, what with all them relations. . . ."

"It wasn't that. It was just the thinking that you were gone, and that I wasn't going to hear the hound music coming down the trail to our house any more."

"I . . . I reckon I'd have come down that trail before very long," said Mississippi. "Of course, after your paw made you promise you wouldn't have nothing to do with me any more. . . ."

"Why, Mississippi, I never promised any such a thing!"

"Why . . . but I thought. . . ."

"You were in the saddle by then. But I told Dad that that was the thing I would *not* promise, ever in the world. Then, after a while, I guessed you had misunderstood . . . and I rode up to your cabin, and you were gone. So I thought I'd just ride along, kind of casual, and pretend . . ." Willa began to cry.

"Shush, there . . . it's all right now, honey child."

"I wouldn't admit the truth to myself, but there's no use fooling any more. I know now I'd rather live with you in a tree than be alive any place else at all."

"Reckon we won't have to live in a tree, hon."

Perhaps her eye caught the glint of the old brasses from that other country that Mississippi was from, for she looked around the room for the first time. A look of puzzlement came into her face as she saw all those surprising things that he had so painstakingly gathered here.

"Mississippi . . . where are we?"

"Home. Home, honey."

The forgotten Thunder Pumper came in wearily and laid a big, mournful head on the edge of the bed.

The Nester's Girl

Tommy Ross, cowhand, brought his buckskin pony to the top of a long rise and reined up. For a few moments he sat quietly while his eyes swept long miles of open country, a vast, brassy land, dotted with creosote bush and limited by a skyline of flat-topped mesas.

Tommy Ross licked dry lips. He was used to being dry himself, but the buckskin pony was showing signs of having missed water the night before, and to ride those long flats on a thirst-racked horse is misery. Two miles downcountry a long rift of willows marked a spot of low, moist ground in the otherwise dust-dry bed of the Blacksnake River. Here a windmill stood, forever pumping cool water from deep down. But the cowboy regarded this oasis with a sardonic eye, for it was enclosed by a sketchy fence, and a squat adobe showed in front of the willow trees.

A year ago this unwary water hole had been landed on by a nester—a lonely, stubborn man who asked no friendship and gave none. Sometimes the range stock, drawn by the smell of water, came to his fences and stood bawling against the wire; the nester had even been known to refuse a man water for his horse. It was tough to ask a favor from this thorn in the side of the range.

Six miles away on his left hand was another water hole—three minutes away by airplane or six by automobile, but a good hour and a half away for a faded horse. Tommy Ross debated. He was a youngster whose quick, very bright blue eyes looked unsquintingly over the desert; his floppy old hat was plastered on one side of his head at a carefree and humorous angle. He did not look like a man about to push his horse six miles to avoid a row with a nester.

By the time he let himself through the slack-wire gate, he had planned out just what he would say: "Kind sir, please, sir, would you have my horse blot up a little water? Or would you sooner see me tie your shotgun around your neck?"

As he approached, he took in the details of the makeshift adobe, sharp-etched by the blasting sun. The roof sloped all one way, to the side, as if its two probable rooms represented only half the house its owner had intended to build, and the door, close under the eaves in a corner, had the cramped look of a door of a chicken coop. Out of this humble dwelling the domestic necessities had overflowed; a bucket and a tub stood on a bench by the door, and the handle of a dipper protruded from the water bucket. He swung down and hammered the door mightily with the loaded butt of his quirt.

The door swung open. "Kind sir, please, sir. . . ."

Tommy's words stuck in his teeth. He had expected the door to be opened by a depraved, shaggy figure in bib overalls. Instead, he confronted a girl in a starched yellow dress. His first thought was that this was the nester's wife—he had heard the fellow had a woman of some kind here—but the picture was all wrong. For this girl was lovely. Her eyes were blue and sparkling and in her golden, tawny skin warm color glowed.

"Excuse me, ma'am," he said, gathering himself. "I didn't go to trouble you. But my horse is right thirsty, and I thought. . . ." He saw with surprise that this girl was afraid of him!

"You shouldn't have come here," she told him sharply. "You people ought to know by this time, my father doesn't allow any cowmen on this place!"

"I don't know," he said gently, "as I ever had the pleasure of meeting up with your father, and I thought. . . ."

"There wouldn't be any pleasure about it," she declared, "either for him or you."

Ross persisted, determined now to get acquainted with this girl. "Ma'am, I wouldn't ask for water for myself. But look at this poor horse, half dead already." The buckskin was now seen to be standing with ears up alertly, and the cowboy surreptitiously bore down on the bit, to make him look low-headed. "You wouldn't refuse a poor dumb animal, ma'am."

The girl's mouth struggled against a smile, and lost. "Take your water. Water your horse and move out."

He immediately turned toward the windmill tank, and behind him he heard the door shut abruptly. Yet he knew that she continued to watch him, and, when his horse had watered, he once more knocked on the door.

"I want to thank you, ma'am. . . ."

"That's all right. Good bye."

"I thought . . . maybe it wouldn't put you out none if I was to rest my pony a little minute, here in the shade. It's awful bad on a horse to put him right on the trail, all newly tanked up."

The color quickened over her cheek bones and he saw that she was not deceived. She hesitated.

"Thank you, ma'am . . . it's appreciated." He squatted on one heel and fell to explaining the state of the grass, afraid that if he ever stopped talking she would close the door. Although he did not look at her directly, he knew when she presently relaxed.

He turned to her. "Seems like . . ."—she looked so pretty standing there he faltered—"seems like you couldn't hardly have been here all the time your pa has, without somebody hearing of you. You just come here lately, didn't you?"

"About four months ago."

"Four months! Don't you ever get to town or anything?"

"No, my father doesn't like the people here. They aren't his kind."

Tommy figured that the nester's hate of cowboys must be a mighty active one to keep his daughter so well hidden. "I suppose," he suggested, "that's why he's gone to town on Monday, instead of Saturday, like most folks."

She nodded. "It isn't hardly necessary for him to go in every week, as he does, but he always wants to get the papers, and see if there's any mail."

Tommy Ross glanced at her to see if she had really meant this to be an invitation but decided not. Suddenly he saw that he had discovered something lovely and desirable and new— and nobody knew about it but himself. An unfamiliar sense of insecurity came over him. It was Tommy's creed that he could ride any horse and kiss any girl, but now he took a short rein on his manners and set about to win the confidence of this girl, and make her like him, little by little.

That day he did not stay long. But as he went over the skyline, he was singing: "I'm just up from Texas, drunk as I can be."

Tommy Ross worked for old Buck Wallace, a cattleman with a genial face of side leather and a mustache of dry grama. Wallace had long ago given up fighting his way rich; in a good year he could make $50,000, and in a bad year lose about the same, and he had learned to take the years as they came. This made him a good man to work for.

His home ranch—a rambling series of adobe structures and strong-built corrals covering a surprising space of ground—always housed five or six cowpunchers, and in work season many more. Of these men Tommy Ross made one

hand. Although one of their principal amusements around
there was swapping lies about their tall adventures, Tommy
kept today's discovery strictly to himself.

It was still his own secret when, on the following Monday,
Ross once more loped down upon the nester's layout. This
time he jumped his pony over the gate and charged the house,
checking at the last possible second to come sliding onto the
doorstep itself. He swung down, grinning, as the girl opened
the door.

"You shouldn't have come back! I *told* you not to come."

He grinned again, hat in hand, and imitated embarrass-
ment. "I know it. But I couldn't help it. I just wanted to see if
you was still here, and all right."

She wavered, but immediately rallied. "I explained to you
how my father is. If he knew you were here. . . ."

"I know. Just another no-good saddle bum, useless,
worthless, and plumb vicious. But I won't be bothering any of
your water. It's only six miles to the next water hole, and. . . ."

"Of course you'll use our water! You know you're perfectly welcome to water. Only my father. . . ."

"Sure, I understand how he looks at it." He knew now that
she had expected him to come back—would have been disappointed if he had not.

Handling their relationship carefully, as if he were trying
to tame a bird, he found out that her name was Ellen. He already knew her father's name was Gunsaulus. What made the
going rough was that her father hated the cattle people implacably. Gingerly Ross tried to find out to what extent the
father had imparted this obsession to the girl.

"Cowpokes and cattlemen are just ordinary fellers trying
to get some beef to market," he tried to tell her. "Socorro
Bass, that you father keeps having run-ins with, he's tough, I
know. But take my own boss, Buck Wallace, a natural-born

181

cowman, and as white a man as ever. . . ."

An unfriendly, combative glow came into her eyes. "A natural-born cowman is a natural-born land hog. He doesn't really use the land . . . he doesn't know how to use it. So to make up he just spreads out all over, grabbing. My father takes only a little tiny piece of land, but he makes every foot of it yield the very best there is in it."

That set Tommy Ross back for a minute, but he stood his ground. "You see all that desert land out there? Put the plow to that land and it blows away. Right here, of course, is a little damp spot, where there's always been water and extra grass . . . and that's the spot your father fences in. You can't call that using the land. It's just skimming the cream. And without this damp spot, fifty square miles of this land is made useless and thrown away. Can he turn off a thousand beeves on this little patch? No, sir! But give me this ground, and I'll use it together with the desert, and I'll get the thousand beeves, all right."

Tommy lost the argument. As a matter of fact, there had originally been no water hole at this point until it was built by the original nester who the rough tactics of Socorro Bass had evicted. So Tommy presently covered up by stating, with only unconscious bravado, that any time her father had trouble with Socorro Bass he would undertake to put Socorro off the place, and Socorro's outfit, too.

The girl's views, however, aroused him to a new curiosity concerning her father. His suggestion that he drop by and meet Gunsaulus only terrified her, but later in the week Ross did come back unannounced, confidently believing that the man didn't live who couldn't be won over to his side.

He found Gunsaulus grubbing away in a garden patch, and, riding up to the fence, he hopefully opened conversation: "Howdy, mister."

Gunsaulus was no more than twenty-five strides away, but he did not reply or turn his head. His hoe swung rhythmically, unchecked. Tommy Ross studied him. Jim Gunsaulus was tall, bent, and gnarled; his hands were misshapen from wrestling with ash-handled tools. He was bearded.

On an impulse, Tommy dropped out of the saddle and crawled through the fence. At this Gunsaulus left his work and walked to a little shed at the end of the patch—promptly to reappear with a shotgun in his hands.

"Get over that fence," he said.

"Look here, Mister Gunsaulus. . . ."

"Get over that fence," Gunsaulus said.

"Look here," Tommy persisted. "You can't haul off and kill a man just for speaking to you in a neighborly way."

"Birdshot won't kill you, I guess. But unless you get off my place right sudden, I sure aim to salt your hide!"

Ross saw the gnarled thumb click the hammer. He turned and walked out of there. On his horse again, he looked back, and he saw that Gunsaulus had resumed hoeing.

Tommy's attitude was that he had given Gunsaulus his chance, and Gunsaulus had passed it up. His next job was to get this girl away from an outrageous father and ride off with her. Ross had little money, but a very thorough knowledge of the jobs and trading chances of the cattle country. He did not fear for the future, once Ellen was at his side.

His first step toward this goal was a canny one. He stayed away from the nester's layout the following week, to give Ellen a chance to wonder. Beyond this he made no plans, and, when he next rode into the nester's layout, he did not mean to stake everything on a single play. But it seemed to him that this time, as she greeted him, she was gentler toward him—even tender, and he instantly knew that Ellen had come by herself to some decision. They sat on the step. Presently he took her hand. Her fingers trembled for an instant, then lay quietly in his hand.

"Tommy . . . I have to tell you something."

He looked at her, but she would not meet his eyes.

"You can't come here any more. It can't go on."

"What's this, now?"

"He can read signs as well as anybody can. He knows that some cowman has come here, every time he's been gone. He got furious, and I had to tell him about . . . your coming here."

"I had hoped," he said, "the question wouldn't come up."

"But it did come up. So last week he stayed home on Monday. You didn't come. But now, when he gets back, he'll know you were here, and he'll . . . I'll have to. . . ."

Ross angered. "If he gets rough with you. . . ."

She shook her head. "It would nearly kill him to think that I *let* you come here. I didn't tell him that. I couldn't."

"So long as it's only me he gets mad at, I guess you can stand it, Ellen."

"He'd kill you! He'd rather see me dead than. . . ."

"Say . . . if you think I'm just going to ride off, out of the picture. . . ."

They sat silently for a moment or two, their eyes in the distance.

"It couldn't go on like this," she repeated.

Looking at her quickly, he saw that her eyes were filled with tears. He turned and took her in his arms, and, as she clung to him, he kissed her temple and the side of her mouth.

"Just you leave it to me," he said. "Old Man Wallace owes me a couple of horses, and those horses are going to take us right on over the next range. You've got your own saddle? Sure. We'll drop down into Salt Fork as we go, and have a word with the justice of the peace, and then. . . ."

Abruptly she freed herself and stood up. "I can't! Tommy, I couldn't ever. . . ."

His hands closed on her shoulders as she tried to turn. "I'll be coming with the saddle stock," he insisted. "Don't bother to pack . . . just stand ready with your saddle and yourself. I'll be here this day week, when he's gone."

"He'll be here. When he finds you've been here. . . ."

"Then I'll be waiting with the horses over there on that skyline mesa. Sometimes you ride these old plugs of his around here. He's used to that. Saddle up and come there, and we'll send his horse home with a note on it."

Ellen was crying, torn to pieces by a cross pull for which there was no compromise. "I don't know," she got out at last. "Go away now. I have to think."

"You'll come," he insisted. "You know you'll come. If you're not there next week, I'll come the week after. Every week, this day, you'll know I'm there."

He rode away then, uncertain whether he had won or lost. He thought she would come, but, if she did not, he was sunk. After that he could only make a fool of himself if he tried loping down into the Gunsaulus layout to make a play square into the nester's beard. If it came to that, he would do better to go over the hill alone, and try to make out to forget her altogether.

Jim Gunsaulus stamped the dust off his flat-heeled boots and came in, and his face was hard as ancient buffalo horn. "So," he said, "he was here again." His daughter, working at the stove, did not answer, and Gunsaulus, changing his coat, went on slowly: "If only he'd come when I'm here. He'd never annoy you again. I'd lesson him! But he won't come, except when I'm gone. Very well, then! I'll leave the town alone. If he. . . ."

Ellen whirled on him unexpectedly. "You can go to town when you like. He's not coming here any more, ever."

"It'll be a good thing if he does not. But I suppose as soon as I set foot off. . . ." Suddenly he stopped, and stood staring at her. "Child," he said at last, "you been crying."

"Well, what of it?"

A terrific anger blazed behind the nester's sun-faded eyes. He seemed to grow bigger, until he looked massive as a silvertip. "If that damn' buckaroo's been bothering you. . . ."

Ellen flared up at him: "Tom Ross never bothered anybody in his life! I told him to go away and not come back, and he won't come back. And I'll never see him again."

Gunsaulus sat down stiffly, and stared at his daughter across the rough table he had made himself. "Child, what's got into you? You gone crazy?"

"Why wouldn't I be crazy? I'm stuck here month in and month out, inside these four walls. You hate everybody so we haven't got a friend in the world, and, if a neighbor stops by, your only thought is your shotgun!"

"Neighbors? We've got no neighbors. By and by other decent people will come, when we've shown the way, and then there'll be no lack of company, nor. . . ."

Ellen turned on her father, and she was pale as buckskin. "I don't care if they never come. There never was a man anywhere, in all the places we've been, that was fit to saddle Tommy's horse, and there'll never be anybody else like him, not to me, if I live a thousand years."

Her father's face was as mottled as his roan beard. Twice in his life, Jim Gunsaulus had been up against cattlemen who were truly hard men. Of these Socorro Bass was one. But it was the other hard one, many years ago, who had originally turned his natural distrust of the saddle-and-rope men to an all-consuming obsession. He used that first unforgivable injustice to squelch his daughter now.

"You've gone wild crazy on me," he said slowly. "I don't know how to handle you any more. If your mother was here, it'd be different. And she'd be here, too, but for cattle."

In a sudden panic Ellen saw what was coming. Jim Gunsaulus was short spoken but, through the words that he only half knew how to use, his bitterness could bear down like the harsh edge of a saw. She wanted to escape, but she did not know how.

"I guess you've forgot Horse Valley," he said. "Yet you was there."

Ellen said in a choked voice: "I remember Horse Valley."

"They cut our fences, and our crops was tromped down. But that was the least. When our grub was gone, and our fires out . . . then your mother was sick. If we could have got her to town, she'd have been all right. But the range hogs had run off our horses. There wasn't any way of getting her that long way through the snow. I dug her grave with these two hands. I mind how hard the ground was . . . it chipped like granite under the pick."

The lesser of the two rooms was Ellen's own, and now she took refuge there and, hiding herself in her bunk, wept unrestrainedly. After a long time her father called to her gently: "Ellen, I got supper on. You best come and eat." But she would not come out.

Jim Gunsaulus was a gentle and kindly man, when the land quarrel was out of his mind; his eyes were dreamer's eyes, and he asked nothing of life but the chance to bring barren land to fertility. All her life those gnarled hands had taken care of Ellen. Whatever she might have wished her own life to be, she could not bring herself to smash up her father.

If it had not been for Socorro Bass, she would have tried to win her father over. But Socorro had not held the Blacksnake

Valley all these years without a stubbornness of his own. He meant to have no interference, nor the beginnings of interference. What means he would take to crush out Gunsaulus, the nester did not know, but certainly he would find means enough. Sometimes, when the father speculated upon the lengths to which Bass might go, Ellen urged him to appeal to the sheriff's office for defense. But nothing could ever persuade Gunsaulus that the injustice of cattlemen might be individual, and not an expression of the breed. "This is a cattle country. The sheriff is a cattleman himself."

Just now Bass seemed to be waiting out the summer—perhaps believing that a sterner discipline would be imposed by letting the nester waste a summer's toil. And meanwhile Ellen was hoping against hope that her father's fear would prove groundless in the end, even that some definite compromise with Bass might weaken her father's prejudice against cowmen.

A week passed by, and two more, and the situation was unchanged. Upon the first Monday after her break with Tommy Ross, Ellen found it all she could do to prevent herself from saddling a horse on impulse and riding off to keep the rendezvous with the cowboy. But she did not. A week later she knew that he had come to the appointed place again, for this time he built a little signal fire that for half the day sent a thin, trailing line of smoke into the sky. That wavering gray line on the sky seemed to Ellen to be pulling her heart out, but she stood fast.

The turn came in the fourth week. For four days a haze of dust far up the Blacksnake had marked a beef roundup in which Socorro's outfit gathered, graded, and cut, preparatory to shipment. On the fifth day Socorro's foreman, Mike Harrison, let his horse through the nester's gate and come jog trotting up to the adobe.

"I haven't any business with you," Gunsaulus said.

"Maybe not, but I have with you," the cow boss told him. "We're driving a little bunch of three hundred head through here tomorrow. We got to weigh them through at the junction, and I don't want to weigh in any dried-out beef. I'm going to have to ask leave to water here tomorrow."

"No," said Gunsaulus. He knew what he was up against well enough. Nobody expected him to give his permission. Not a stick of Kaffir corn or anything else would be standing, once the bars were down and the herd through. "No," he said again, "you'll water no cattle here."

Mike Harrison spoke casually, like a reasonable man: "We've stood a lot from you, Gunsaulus. If I was you, I wouldn't get tough about a little water at a special time."

"You'll water no stock," said Gunsaulus again.

"I've told you what we're going to do," Mike Harrison said with careful clarity. "My drive will be here tomorrow noon. Think it over, Gunsaulus."

The nester suddenly angered. He reached into the doorway and the shotgun appeared, cradled across his left arm. "It's my place you're standing on, and it's my right to tell you to get off. Now you get gone."

Mike Harrison smiled, spat, and jogged down to the gate. This time, however, he did not dismount. He leaned low in his saddle and with his wire nippers cut the two top strands of the fence, and hopped his horse over the remaining wire. Jim Gunsaulus whipped up his shotgun and fired.

As he had told Tommy Ross, he was carrying a birdshot load. Yet now Ellen saw Socorro's range boss slur sideways out of his saddle and hit the ground as his stung pony jumped from under. The pony, checked by the reins which Harrison still gripped, snorted and braced his legs as it stood above the fallen man. And for almost a full minute Harrison lay quietly, while Ellen thought the man was dead.

Harrison stirred at last. He got to his feet, and then gingerly into the saddle—and rode away.

"He had no gun," Gunsaulus said. "He thought he could make free with me because he had no gun."

He did not look at his daughter; his face was set as hard as concrete. Both of them knew without discussion what they had come to. Gunsaulus, being what he was, could not yield, and Socorro Bass, with his mounted men and trampling cattle, held the whip hand.

The crisis came sooner than the nester had supposed. The cattle could only move slowly, but horsemen could drift across the face of the desert at any old gait. And now, at mid-morning, four mounted men appeared, not from up the Blacksnake, but squarely out of the west.

Buck Wallace had sent Tommy Ross ahead to a point where he could watch the nester's layout and with other three cowboys had dismounted behind the long rise. But now Tommy Ross came loping back.

"Socorro's coming along now, Mister Wallace. Him and four others are drifting in, close along the Blacksnake, about two miles out. I don't believe Gunsaulus can see them yet."

"Who's he got with him, Tommy?" Ross, with the desert man's ability to recognize a particular horse or man as far as the figure can be seen, named the men with Sirocco, and Wallace seemed satisfied. "We'll be going down there now."

They mounted and moved over the rise at a dog-trot. Ross said: "I better go on ahead."

"Might's well. Mind you, it's your job to keep the nester from spilling the beans. Don't pay any attention to me and Socorro unless the guns come out. But I don't think there'll be anything like that."

Ross shot ahead and loped down upon the nester's layout. As he rode, he stood up in his stirrups and waved his hat. What he had not told his boss was that he set all his hope of keeping the nester peaceable on having a word with Ellen first. A few hundred yards away Tommy drew his horse to a walk and came on quietly, and, as he closed the distance, Ellen presently left the house and walked toward him.

Tommy swung down, and faced the girl across the gate. "Where's your father?"

"He's asleep."

"Glory on the ridges! Tell you what you do. . . ."

"You have to go away," she told him desperately. "You haven't any right to come here!"

"And leave you to face the music? That's a hot one."

"There isn't any music to face. There isn't anything wrong here! Now, are you going to get out of here or not?"

"Not," he said. "I heard the whole dope in town. I told you I'd chase Socorro home, if he bothered you, and now you'll see me do it. Will you paddle right on up to the house and get me your father's shotgun, or shall I go get it myself?"

Suddenly the stiffness of Ellen's determination seemed to leave her. She turned and went toward the house. He waited hopefully, but sailed his hat away in a gesture of magnificent relief when she finally put the gun in his hands.

He hid it in the grass under the fence. "Now we'll just go up to the house and take a grandstand seat on the stoop."

"We'll . . . we'll wake up my father!"

"Well, he can't sleep forever. But I'll be quiet."

They sat on the step, the girl tremulous, the cowboy elated. He linked his left arm through hers and held both of her hands in his left. But she did not fail to notice the sagging gun belt that she had never before seen him wear.

Buck Wallace and his two cowpunchers had reached the

fence by now. They drifted along it and took a post close to the bed of the Blacksnake, fifty yards from the house.

Then from beyond the Blacksnake willows Socorro Bass and his boys appeared, wolf-trotting their ponies. They saluted Buck Wallace and his cowboys gravely, without surprise; obviously they had seen Wallace approach from a long way. A few rods more they drew up, and Socorro stepped his horse forward, alone.

"Howdy, Socorro."

"Howdy, Buck."

"You may as well keep your boys in their saddles, Socorro. There isn't going to be any wire cut."

Socorro's voice raised, soft-edged but chesty: "Now, you wait a minute, Buck. I don't come fretting your range, and you. . . ."

Within the house, boot heels hit the floor abruptly; a chair tipped over. Ellen sprang up, and Tommy, rising less hurriedly, stepped clear of the door.

Ellen cried out: "He . . . he's . . . !"

Gunsaulus filled the doorway, red-eyed and bristling, like a trapped bear. "Ellen," he bellowed, "where's my gun?" Then his eyes fell on Ross, and for an instant his jaw dropped. "You damned. . . ."

"Listen," said Tommy, watching Buck Wallace. "Listen a minute!"

Gunsaulus disappeared from the door and for a moment seemed to be rummaging furiously.

"Ellen, my gun's gone! If I lay hands on that gun. . . ."

His daughter cried out frantically—"Will you listen?"—and for a moment Gunsaulus was still.

From his post fifty yards away the voice of Buck Wallace came, clear and distinct; he did not interest himself in the disturbance behind him: "You know I'm deputy sheriff in this

county, Socorro. And I've got a writ of injunction from Judge
Stacker forbidding you to cut this wire . . . or in any other way
molest, interfere with, or crowd in on this little helpless
feller."

Socorro's legs stiffened, raising him in the saddle so that
he seemed to swell. His face was discolored. "Buck . . ."—his
voice rose slowly, with a suppressed power behind it like the
wind that sweeps across the flat land—"Buck, from time to
time I've stood a lot from you, but there comes a time. . . ."

Buck Wallace cut in, his voice matter-of-fact. "I was sure
hoping we wouldn't have any words, Socorro. As a matter of
fact, in riding over this way, I was kind of figuring we might
get together on me selling you that other water hole of mine
that you've been wanting."

Socorro Bass paused and sat for a long moment staring at
Buck Wallace. A moment before he had been in a position
from which, with his men watching him, he could not retreat.
Never in the turbulent history of the Blacksnake had two men
been closer to gunsmoke. But now Buck Wallace had shifted
the precarious balance of the deadlock in the one safe way; he
had offered Socorro Bass a back way out.

"At my own price?" said Socorro at last.

"At the last price you offered," Buck Wallace amended.

Once more Socorro hesitated; he could do nothing else
but hesitate, if he were to save his face. "It's a deal I can't
hardly pass up," he finally admitted. "I'm not making any
promises on this nester thing. But I'll say this . . . I'm willing
to put this thing here off until we close up that other water-
hole deal."

"I understand that, Socorro." But they knew Socorro Bass
had accepted his way out.

Ellen Gunsaulus put her hands over her face and swayed
with the slackness that comes suddenly when lightning has

struck close to you, but passed you by, and Tommy Ross steadied her. She hid her face against his brush jacket, her shoulders shaking, and Ross looked inquiringly over her head at Gunsaulus.

The nester stood, blank-faced, his eyes bewildered. His hands hung helplessly at his side, like sawbucks hung up by rope. "Mister," said Ross, "could you tell me what she's crying about?"

Gunsaulus looked at the two of them, but without apparent comprehension. Then he turned and went into his house, walking like a man stunned.

Tommy Ross was startled by Ellen's muffled whisper: "How's he taking it?"

"He'll be all right. We ain't got him gentled, but I guess he's broke to stake."

One of Buck's cowboys was mending the wire Mike Harrison had cut.

Fight at Painted Rock

Gar Lacey once rode with Billy the Kid for about four days, and it made such an impression on him that he imitated the Kid all the rest of his short life. He did a good job of it; some thought his later gun play was smokier than the Kid's own.

When Gar was killed, at the age of twenty-two, he had filed seventeen notches on his gun, conscientiously not counting the little colored boy he killed by mistake at Alamogordo, or the old lady who ill-advisedly tried to sell tortillas in the line of fire at Las Cruces. Some of the notches were for fighting men who were plenty tough, and all of the notches were honest—except one.

Gar himself never knew that one of the notches tallied a man who was still alive. If he had known it, he would have felt humiliated. Probably he would have gone out and shot a Mexican or somebody, to bring the tally up to scratch. The phony notch was for a cowboy by the name of Tommy Roddy who Gar Lacey had fought in Painted Rock. He would have been dead; he had every reason to be dead; a score had seen him shot, not once but many times, and had seen him fall. It was not Gar Lacey's fault that this one simply would not die.

There were other things about that fight that Gar Lacey never knew. He knew nothing about the gunfighting marshal of Painted Rock, a man who might have had a chance against Gar, as Tommy Roddy certainly did not, yet who sent Tommy Roddy in against him and himself stayed away. Especially Gar would have been surprised to hear that this fight was over a girl of whom he had never seen or heard.

Except for her, the shoot-out wouldn't have amounted to

much, as shoot-outs went, for Tommy Roddy had made no name as a gunfighter. He hadn't made a name as anything. He wasn't even the sort of youngster who belonged in Painted Rock at all.

Painted Rock consisted mainly of one rickety street of false-fronted bars and blamed its existence on a cattle trail that gathered herds from a vast, thin land. It was surrounded on both sides and part of the top by a lot of highly colored scenery, of a kind very hard on horses' hoofs. The inhabitants didn't appreciate the scenery very much. They would have liked a few more different flavors of beans, a few more good-looking women, and some grub without any sand in it, in trade for several hundred square miles of assorted views.

Tommy Roddy looked very much like any trail-town loafer with a saddle and no horse. Until he played his mouth organ, you couldn't tell him from the others. But when he sat on his back and made the mouth organ sing and cry, you knew he was a long way from where he belonged. What usually came out of the mouth organ was pure river country. If you were from the river, it took you back there so plainly that you forgot where you were. You could hear Negro voices in the mouth-organ reeds, the dancing bare feet of darkies slapping on the planks, and the rough-throated moan of boat whistles far downstream. The baked smell of the desert turned into the smell of lazy running water, cotton bales, and catfish frying, and the dust of distant herds became the river mists, walking on smooth water at twilight. Until at last you could see the brown Mississippi, a mile wide and brimming, swinging down the long bends between its plantations and its woods.

Tommy Roddy had wandered westward through a hundred cow camps for no better reason than a legion like him could have given; there were plenty more like Tommy Roddy on the Western trails. Finally he had wandered into Painted Rock and there, having set eyes on Nancy Plain, had failed to wander on.

Nancy Plain lived with her brother Judd, who also had wandered into Painted Rock not so very long before, and stayed on because he had promoted himself into a pretty good thing as town marshal. Except that Nancy was there, Tommy Roddy had no earthly business in Painted Rock. There wasn't anything there for him to do. As his money dribbled away, he took to swamping bars for drinks or a meal, no better off than any other saddle bum waiting for a herd to come through and pick him up. Only Tommy Roddy let the herds drift on through without him.

Marshal Judd Plain could have helped him get something if he had been of a mind to, but he wasn't of a mind to. Between these two men there was less than ten years difference in age, but Judd could hardly have reached thirty, yet one of them seemed young and the other old.

Judd Plain had a great solidarity, like pie for breakfast, or a pair of bricks. It was in his shoulders, which were a little warped but very strong, and in the set of his heels, which planted themselves as if he were liable to take root any time now. And especially it was in his eyes, old beyond his years. It made him a good marshal, one who seldom had to draw a gun. Just about every night during that blazing hot summer Tommy Roddy was to be found gone to roost on the gallery of the Plains' little house, out toward the end of Painted Rock's single street. He made no special play at Nancy. How could he? Except for his saddle, he didn't have a thing.

But along about the time of evening, when the cub coyotes would begin tuning up out in the sand hills, Tommy Roddy would be warming up the mouth organ on the Plain gallery.

Both tune-ups sounded almost alike to Judd Plain, who objected to Roddy's making noises like that at his sister, but hardly knew what to do about it. For Tommy Roddy could make the mouth organ talk on topics other than the Mississippi River. He could make it sing about exiled, homesick youngsters wandering over endless badlands in search of something they could not name. He could make it sing about a man finding what he was looking for, and knowing it when he saw it, even though he had never known what it was before, and then not knowing what to do about it, because he had empty pockets and empty hands.

That mouth organ could break your heart with the realization that it wasn't ever going to do you any good to move on any more, while at the same time you couldn't bear to stay where you were. And sometimes the mouth organ talked much plainer than that, so that Nancy blushed under cover of the dark, strangely disturbed by the pulse of the reeds, and her brother would shift his shoulders restlessly, resentful, but not knowing how to stop this thing.

Judd Plain wanted his sister to send Tommy packing. "This Roddy guy is worse useless," he complained, "than window shades on a horse. He's more useless than a nightshirt on a hog. Nance, stick a road brand on this maverick. Spank him one with a pair of cactus, and let's have him on his way!"

"How can I do that? He hasn't said anything to me."

"He better hadn't, too."

So the summer ran along, with the Mississippi magic of the mouth organ's moaning out its soul, until often Nancy couldn't sleep and didn't want to, and all three of them knew that something would have to break. Tommy Roddy knew the break, all right, when it came.

It was dusk, and Tommy Roddy had moved in on the Plain

gallery, slow-going, casual, apologetic, as he always looked, and the mouth organ was beginning to tune up.

"You ain't wearing no gun, I see," the marshal said.

Tommy Roddy shook his head with a slow, absent motion, not stopping the wail of his mouth organ, then let it drift from his lips long enough to say: "I've got no dispute on with anybody, not that I know."

Judd Plain, marshal of Painted Rock, stood up and went into the house, spurless boots clomping. He was gone several minutes. When he came out on the low gallery again, he had in his hands a gun belt not his own.

Tommy Roddy was sitting on the small of his back on the gallery floor, his propped-up knees crossed and his shoulders braced against the house wall.

"I'll lend you this here gun," the marshal said, holding out the holster to Tommy Roddy. "Other day, you said you wanted a chance. Here it is. I'm giving you one."

Judd Plain's voice was flat and level. No hidden meaning showed in his still face, or in his hand and steady eyes. But contempt was there, although it was hidden. Tommy knew it, and Judd Plain knew he knew it, and the girl, sitting in the shadows, understood them both.

Tommy became so still that he didn't even put the mouth organ down. He just sat there as if he were suddenly turned to wood, except for his eyes. His eyes rolled upward with a slow inquiry to the figure of the marshal, standing over him in the dusk.

Judd tossed a shiny piece of nickel plate into Tommy Roddy's lap.

"That's a deputy badge. Stick it on your shirt. This here's the key to the Home for Disorderly."

He threw a great, foolish piece of ironwork on the floor beside Tommy. It thundered down like a crowbar falling—a rusty, ancient key to a lock you could have picked with a horseshoe.

"There's a kid cowboy raising hell in Dunfree's place," the marshal said. "You go on down. Go down there and pick up this drunk kid, and sling him in the trap."

Tommy Roddy said thoughtfully: "Kind of a slim boy, with yaller hair?"

"Oh, you saw him already?"

"Yes, I saw him as I come by Dunfree's."

"That's the one."

Tommy didn't move right away. After a moment or two he put the mouth organ back to his lips and played a few more bars. But there was no more rhythm to it, and the wail trailed off into silence.

"Go pick him up," Judd Plain said again. "You asked for a chance, didn't you? What are you waiting for?"

Tommy Roddy was looking at Nancy through the thickening dusk, but she would not meet his eyes. She knew he wanted her to say something. Anything would have been better than nothing at all. She could have said—"Do it, Tommy."—or—"Don't you do it."—anything. But she didn't speak, or look at him.

Tommy Roddy wiped the mouth organ on his sleeve and put it in his pocket. He pinned the plated badge on his shirt; it shone very bright and new, even in the twilight, against the wash-worn flannel. He stood up and took the gun belt in his hands.

Nothing was readable in his face as he buckled on the leather. Only, his hands were very slow—too slow, too careful, as if his fingers were hindered by the fading of the light. When he had stepped off the gallery, he turned back to Nancy.

He said: "I . . ."—and fumbled. "I. . . ." At last he just

said—"Well, so long."—and turned away.

Nancy said—"Good luck, Tommy."—very low, so low that perhaps he didn't hear her. Or perhaps he didn't answer because in her hushed tone there was pity of a kind that neither Tommy Roddy nor any man in Painted Rock that night would have liked to take. He went down the boardwalk toward the riotous heart of the raw, one-streeted town.

"Yellow," Judd Plain said in that flat, steady tone of his with its east Texas slur. "Yellow to the bones."

Nancy said: "There never was a sweeter man. You can't imagine Tommy Roddy ever doing a mean thing, or a cheap thing, or a small one."

"That don't count."

The girl got up and went inside. The marshal took the rocker she had left, and sat smoking with the slack, idle hands of a man entirely at rest.

Tommy Roddy walked on down along the hitch rails where the lines of ponies stood, past the bleak-faced bars with their small-paned, bright-lighted windows. There was plenty of noise going on in most of them, but in Dunfree's place, although there were plenty of customers, the crowd was quiet. A slim, blond youngster with thick-lidded eyes was at the head of the bar. He was beginning to sway on his elbows, but his eyes were active under their heavy lids.

Experience had taught the customers the signs. The kid was waiting for a ruckus, and would have it before he was through. They stayed to see it, although no one as yet wanted to take part in it exactly.

Nobody paid any attention to Tommy Roddy as he came in, looking slow, casual, and apologetic, as usual. There was a little clear space that by common consent had been left along the bar next to the blond kid, and Tommy slid into this.

After a moment Tommy Roddy said: "Look. Look. I've got to take you in."

The kid at the bar looked blank, surprised. "What did you say?" And Roddy told him again.

The cowboy stared at Roddy, and, after a moment, he began to smile. It was a thin-lipped smile, but lively and happy. "Well," he said, "why don't you do it?"

Unhurried, he turned to the bar, and tossed his whiskey down. Roddy just waited. He acted as if he didn't know how to go about this job, or what to do.

Then suddenly the kid at the bar snapped around to face Roddy, and his gun was in his hand, although nobody had seen him draw. He still looked pleased, but the thin-lipped smile was gone from his face.

"You get the hell out of here," he said.

Tommy Roddy answered: "I just can't do it, Gar."

Until that moment no one in the bar had recognized Gar Lacey. Probably only one or two of the quick ones recognized him now. But later, when they learned who the blond kid was, they remembered that Tommy Roddy had stood there and called him by name.

"I just can't," Tommy Roddy said again. And he jerked his gun.

One gun roared, and it wasn't Roddy's. Tommy Roddy slumped forward and went down. His unfired gun rattled freely against the foot rail, and his face struck the floor undefended.

The kid at the bar kept his gun in his hand. "One more whiskey," he said, and the pop-eyed bartender slopped full the glass.

The kid was suddenly sober now, and very cool. The place was so quiet that the men along the wall could hear one another breathe.

In that sudden quiet the fallen man began to move. Tommy Roddy tried to get his legs under him, but he could not. He got hold of his gun again, though. He turned on one elbow, and raised the gun.

Without any change in his face the kid at the bar fired twice more. Some of the watchers winced a little, each in his own way. They didn't so much mind gun play, but it went against them to see the lead pour into a downed man. They figured afterward that those two shots broke Roddy's right arm and right shoulder, but by the way he collapsed they thought at the moment that he was killed.

The kid cowboy drank his whiskey, and he eyed the fallen man curiously as his quick fingers reloaded the fired chambers of his gun. Then he stepped around Roddy, and backed out onto the walk.

The cowmen who had flattened against the wall relaxed a little, and a couple of them were swearing softly to themselves. Then something happened in there that their eyes couldn't believe.

Tommy Roddy was getting up.

He got to his knees, groping crazily, and his left hand got hold of his gun once more. There were bubbles at his lips, but somehow he pitched to his feet. Almost at the door he stumbled and went to his knees, but the side of the door caught him, and once more his gun came up.

The kid who had shot him was swinging onto his pony out there. They heard him cuss as Roddy's gun spoke at last. The kid fired twice more, cracking the steel to his pony as he fired. His last shot, got off as the pony jumped, went wildly through the window, and broke a whiskey jug. It was the only one that missed. And Tommy Roddy was down again, this time to stay.

Instantly, as soon as the gunfighting kid was definitely

pouring hoof thunder down the street, the crowd that had backed up against the wall closed in around the fallen man. Doc Chance, who always lit out at a high lope, probe in hand, at the sound of gunfire, came forcing his way in, shouting futilely for them to stand back.

There was some confusion of voices, and hauling this way and that, as they tried to decide where Tommy Roddy should be taken. But now Judd Plain came shouldering through. The marshal was not looking himself. It was the first time any of them had seen him look scared, let alone bewildered. At his orders they carried Tommy to Judd's own house.

Then, as half the town milled around in front of Judd Plain's house to talk it over, the true name of the gunfighting blond kid spread through the crowd: "Gar Lacey! That was Gar Lacey!"

In five minutes everyone in Painted Rock knew that Tommy Roddy had walked in against one of the deadliest cases of gun lightning then abroad in the West. Gar Lacey! The fastest man in town would have wanted no part of him.

Nancy Plain went in then to where Doc was finishing his work, although Doc Chance had ordered her out of there. Tommy lay quietly, his eyes dull in a bloodless face, but Nancy was flustered and incoherent:

"Tommy, I brought in your mouth organ. It . . . it fell in the street."

"I missed him," Tommy said vaguely. His eyes wandered. "I could see him plain, and I failed."

"Tommy, Tommy," Nancy said, "you didn't fail! You had no chance! Do you know who that was? That was Gar Lacey! Gar Lacey . . . do you understand?"

Tommy did not speak, but Doc Chance said: "Well, he knows it. He knew it all the time."

"He . . . he knew Gar Lacey . . . and yet he . . . ?"

"Heck, Tommy even called him by name, there at the bar."

Nancy stared at him. "But . . . but . . . Judd thought. . . ." Suddenly her face went blank and stricken. The mouth organ fell from her hands; it teetered for a moment on the edge of the cot where Tommy Roddy lay, then clattered to the floor. "Then he thinks that Judd . . . he thinks that we . . . Tommy, look at me! We didn't know! It isn't true!"

Tommy Roddy looked at her squarely, yet without seeming to see her, then, deliberately, he turned his face to the wall.

Nancy went back to her brother. "Judd, he knew! He knew it was Gar Lacey all the time!"

The marshal was still looking dazed, but his eyes snapped hard to her face. "Uhn-uh. He wouldn't've gone into it if . . . wait. Maybe he would, at that. Yes, I guess he would, to judge by what he went and done."

"Judd, he thinks you *knew!* He thinks we both knew, and just sent him in, knowing!"

Judd slowly considered that. "No," he decided. "No. He couldn't think that. Nobody could think that. Why, that would've been common murder."

Nancy's words were quick and contemptuous. "He thinks we counted on him to quit. He thinks we did it to show him up and be rid of him. We gave him a choice of being shown up or killed . . . as clear as that!"

"Well," her brother said slowly, "I reckon that's just about what we done. But don't just go blaming me! You knew I aimed to show him up, even if we didn't know it was Gar. And you just set there and never hollered. You're as much to blame as me!"

"I'm not blaming you. I'm blaming myself. I'm hating myself as I never knew I could hate anything." Her voice was small and blurred. "I'll make it up to him. I'll spend my whole life making it up to him, if only. . . ."

Doc Chance, who had joined them in time to hear the last of that, said: "Heck, I never see such a lucky stiff. Why is it some jiggers go through life hounded with luck, and the rest of us just have to grind along with collections like they is?"

"You mean he isn't killed?"

"I don't know how come there's no way to demolish him, but seemingly there ain't. He'll come up a-rarin' . . . he's going to be all right."

"He'll never forgive me," Nancy whispered. "He'll never forgive me, so long as he lives. He . . . he turned his face to the wall, so he wouldn't have to look at me. What's that?"

A queer, thin quaver of sound was coming from the room where Tommy Roddy lay.

"Why," Judd Plain said, "that sure sounds like . . . yes, sir, it is! Nancy, that unstoppable feller has gone back to mooing through the mouth organ again already! Of all the eternal damnation things I ever seen, this beats. . . ."

"Somebody ought to take that thing away from him," Doc said. "He's got no business blowing through that. Somebody ought to. . . ."

Clear and plain, plainer than words could be, the mouth organ was calling Nancy back. Nancy's head came up, her eyes suddenly bright. "You leave it to me! I'll fix him!" They stood back, and let her take over.

Yet, when she came near him, it was Tommy who did most of the talking, little breath as he had. "I heard all that," he told her. "I did think you knew it was Gar. But I didn't ever believe you wanted me killed. You know what I thought? I thought *you* believed I could take him, Nancy."

One wavering hand got the mouth organ to his lips again, but she took it away from him.

"Look," he said. "Look. I can take him. I can trail him down, and this time I'll beat him. I can get him for you, Nancy, if you want."

"What in the world would I want with a dead gunman?" Nancy was crying a little. She was mighty sick of Painted Rock, just then. Running through her head was a lazy confusion of tunes that were full of river mists, the chant of Negro deck hands, and the smell of fresh-ginned cotton. "Hush, now," she told Tommy. "I'll tell you later what it is I want."

About the Author

Alan LeMay was born in Indianapolis, Indiana, and attended Stetson University in DeLand, Florida, in 1916. Following his military service, he completed his education at the University of Chicago. His short story, "Hullabaloo," appeared the month of his graduation in *Adventure* (6/30/22). He was a prolific contributor to the magazine markets in the mid-1920s. With the story, "Loan of a Gun," LeMay broke into the pages of *Collier's* (2/23/29). During the next decade he wanted nothing more than to be a gentleman rancher, and his income from writing helped support his enthusiasms which included tearing out the peach-tree orchard so he could build a polo field on his ranch outside Santee, California. It was also during this period that he wrote some of his most memorable Western novels, *Gunsight Trail* (1931), *Winter Range* (1932), *Cattle Kingdom* (1933), and *Thunder in the Dust* (1934) among them. In the late 1930s he was plunged into debt because of a divorce and turned next to screenwriting, early attaching himself to Cecil B. DeMille's unit at Paramount Pictures. LeMay continued to write original screenplays through the 1940s, and on one occasion even directed the film based on his screenplay.

The Searchers (1954) is regarded by many as LeMay's masterpiece. It possesses a graphic sense of place; it etches deeply the feats of human endurance that LeMay tended to admire in the American spirit; and it has that characteristic suggestiveness of tremendous depths and untold stories developed in his long apprenticeship writing short stories. A subtext often rides on a snatch of dialogue or flashes in a laconic observation. It was followed by such classic Western novels as *The Unforgiven* (1957) and *By Dim and Flaring Lamps* (1962). *Mustang Breed* will be Alan LeMay's next **Five Star Western**.

Additional copyright information:

"Whack-Ear's Pup" first appeared in *Adventure* (10/30/25). Copyright © 1925 by The Ridgway Company. Copyright © renewed 1953 by Alan LeMay. Copyright © 2004 by the Estate of Alan LeMay for restored material.

"Strange Fellows" first appeared under the title "Strange Fellers" in *Adventure* (12/20/25). Copyright © 1925 by The Ridgway Company. Copyright © renewed 1953 by Alan LeMay. Copyright © 2004 by the Estate of Alan LeMay for restored material.

"Gunnies from Gehenna" under the byline Alan M. Emley first appeared in *Popular Western* (2/36). Copyright © 1936 by Beacon Magazines, Inc. Copyright © renewed 1964 by the Estate of Alan LeMay. Copyright © 2004 by the Estate of Alan LeMay for restored material.

"Hard-Boiled" under the byline Alan M. Emley first appeared in *Popular Western* (4/36). Copyright © 1936 by Beacon Magazines, Inc. Copyright © renewed 1964 by the Estate of Alan LeMay. Copyright © 2004 by the Estate of Alan LeMay for restored material.

"Next Door to Hell" under the byline Alan M. Emley first appeared in *Western Action Novels* (9/36). Copyright © 1936 by Winford Publications, Inc. Copyright © renewed 1964 by the Estate of Alan LeMay. Copyright © 2004 by the Estate of Alan LeMay for restored material.

"Feud Fight" first appeared in *Collier's* (3/23/40). Copyright © 1940 by The Crowell-Collier Publishing Company. Copyright © renewed 1968 by the Estate of Alan LeMay. Copyright © 2004 by the Estate of Alan LeMay for restored material.

"Thanks to a Girl in Love" first appeared in *Collier's* (4/16/32). Copyright © 1932 by P. F. Collier & Son, Inc. Copyright © renewed 1960 by Alan LeMay. Copyright © 2004 by the Estate of Alan LeMay for restored material.

"Man with a Future" first appeared in *Collier's* (7/3/37). Copyright © 1937 by P. F. Collier & Son, Inc. Copyright © renewed 1965 by the Estate of Alan LeMay. Copyright © 2004 by the Estate of Alan LeMay for restored material.

"Old Thunder Pumper" first appeared in *Collier's* (3/22/30). Copyright © 1930 by P. F. Collier & Son, Inc. Copyright © renewed 1958 by Alan LeMay. Copyright © 2004 by the Estate of Alan LeMay for restored material.

"The Nester's Girl" first appeared in *Collier's* (2/11/33). Copyright © 1933 by P. F. Collier & Son, Inc. Copyright © renewed 1961 by the Estate of Alan LeMay. Copyright © 2004 by the Estate of Alan LeMay for restored material.

"Fight at Painted Rock" first appeared in *Collier's* (5/6/39). Copyright © 1939 by The Crowell-Collier Publishing Company. Copyright © renewed 1967 by the Estate of Alan LeMay. Copyright © 2004 by the Estate of Alan LeMay for restored material.